B.U.

GN

STONE ARCH BOOKS
a capstone imprint

STONE ARCH BOOKS™

Published in 2015 by Stone Arch Books
A Capstone Imprint
1710 Roe Crest Drive
North Mankato, MN 56003
www.capstonepub.com

Originally published by DC Comics in the U.S. in single
magazine form as Batman: Li'l Gotham #7.
Copyright © 2015 DC Comics. All Rights Reserved.

DC Comics
1700 Broadway, New York, NY 10019
A Warner Bros. Entertainment Company
No part of this publication may be reproduced in
whole or in part, or stored in a retrieval system, or
transmitted in any form or by any means, electronic,
mechanical, photocopying, recording, or otherwise,
without written permission.

Cataloging-in-Publication Data is available at the
Library of Congress website:
ISBN: 978-1-4342-9666-5 (library binding)

Printed in China by Nordica.
0914/CA21401510
092014   008470NORDS15

Summary: During Japan's Month of Waters, Aquaman
calls upon The Dark Knight, so get ready for a battle of
GIGANTIC proportions as the Bat-family faces robots,
sea monsters, and more. Then, on Independence Day,
Uncle Sam implores his villainous friends to steal all the
fireworks for one explosive celebration!

STONE ARCH BOOKS
Ashley C. Andersen Zantop **Publisher**
Michael Dahl **Editorial Director**
Sean Tulien **Editor**
Heather Kindseth **Creative Director**
Bob Lentz **Art Director**
Hilary Wacholz and Peggie Carley **Designers**
Tori Abraham **Production Specialist**

DC Comics
Kristy Quinn **Original U.S. Editor**

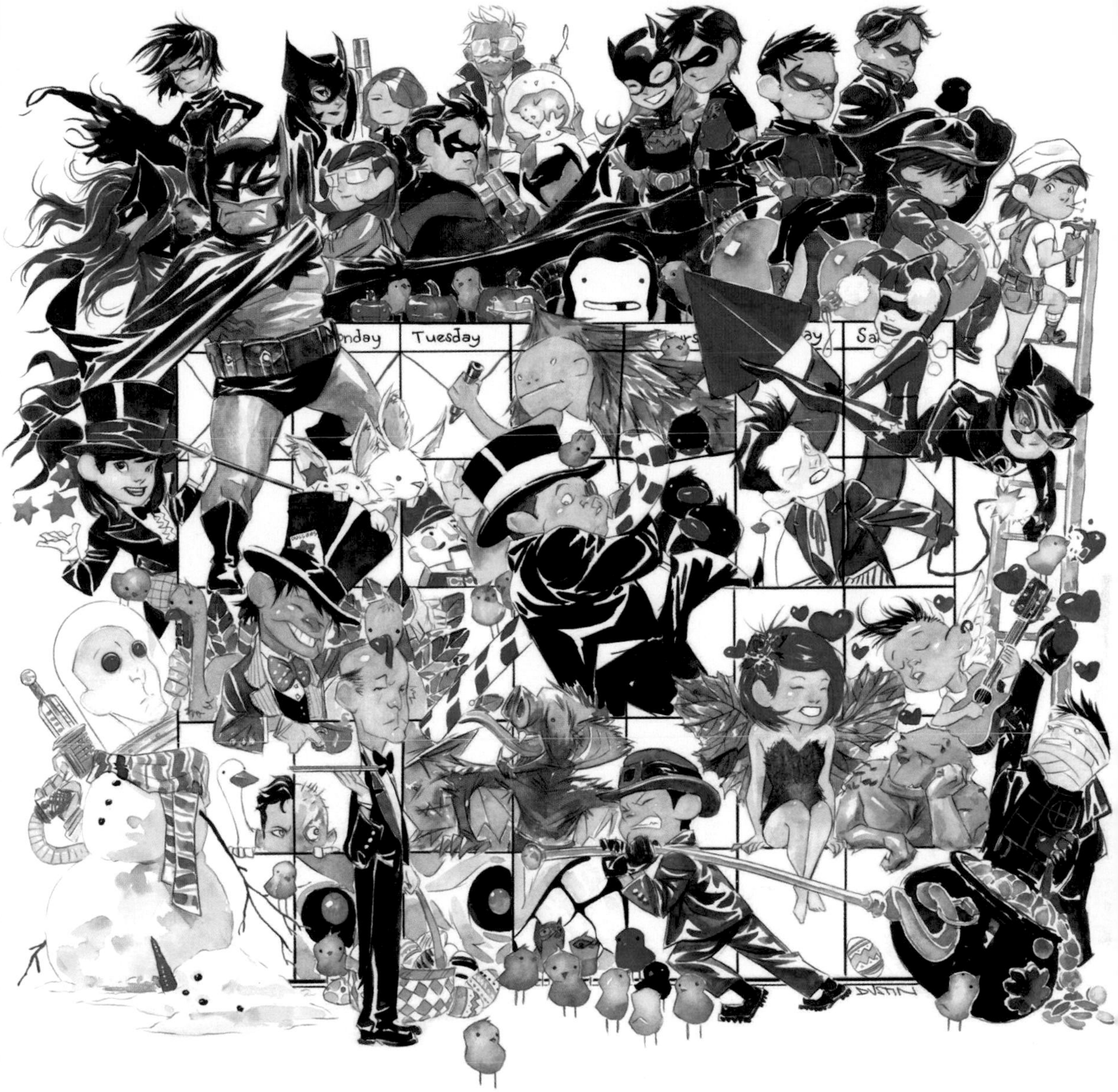
Tuesday
DUSTIN

MONTH OF WATERS AND INDEPENDENCE DAY

Dustin Nguyen and Derek Fridolfs .... writers
Dustin Nguyen.. artist
Saida Temofonte.. letterer

BATMAN created by
Bob Kane

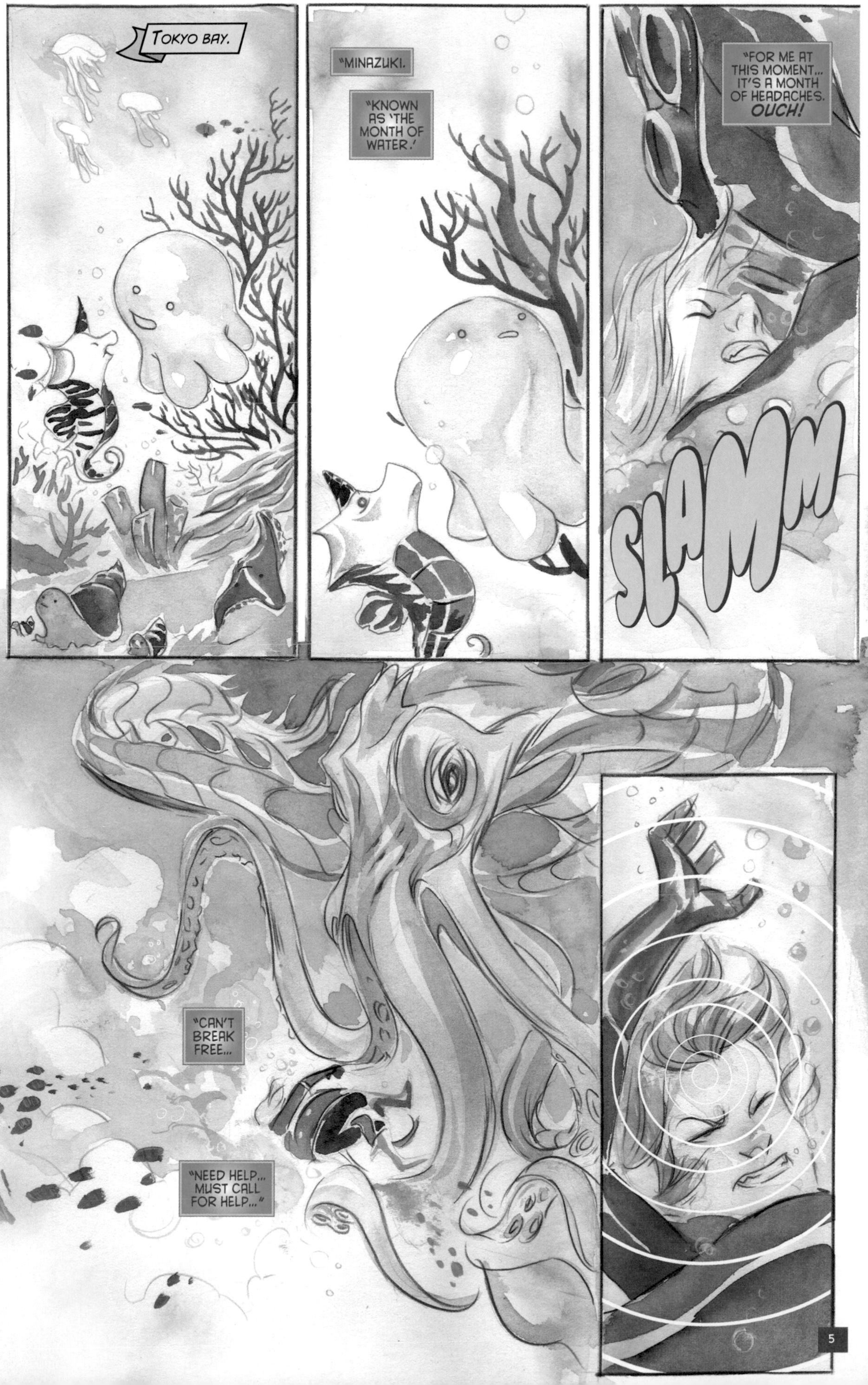
TOKYO BAY.
"MINAZUKI.
"KNOWN AS 'THE MONTH OF WATER.'
"FOR ME AT THIS MOMENT... IT'S A MONTH OF HEADACHES. OUCH!
SLAMM
"CAN'T BREAK FREE...
"NEED HELP... MUST CALL FOR HELP..."

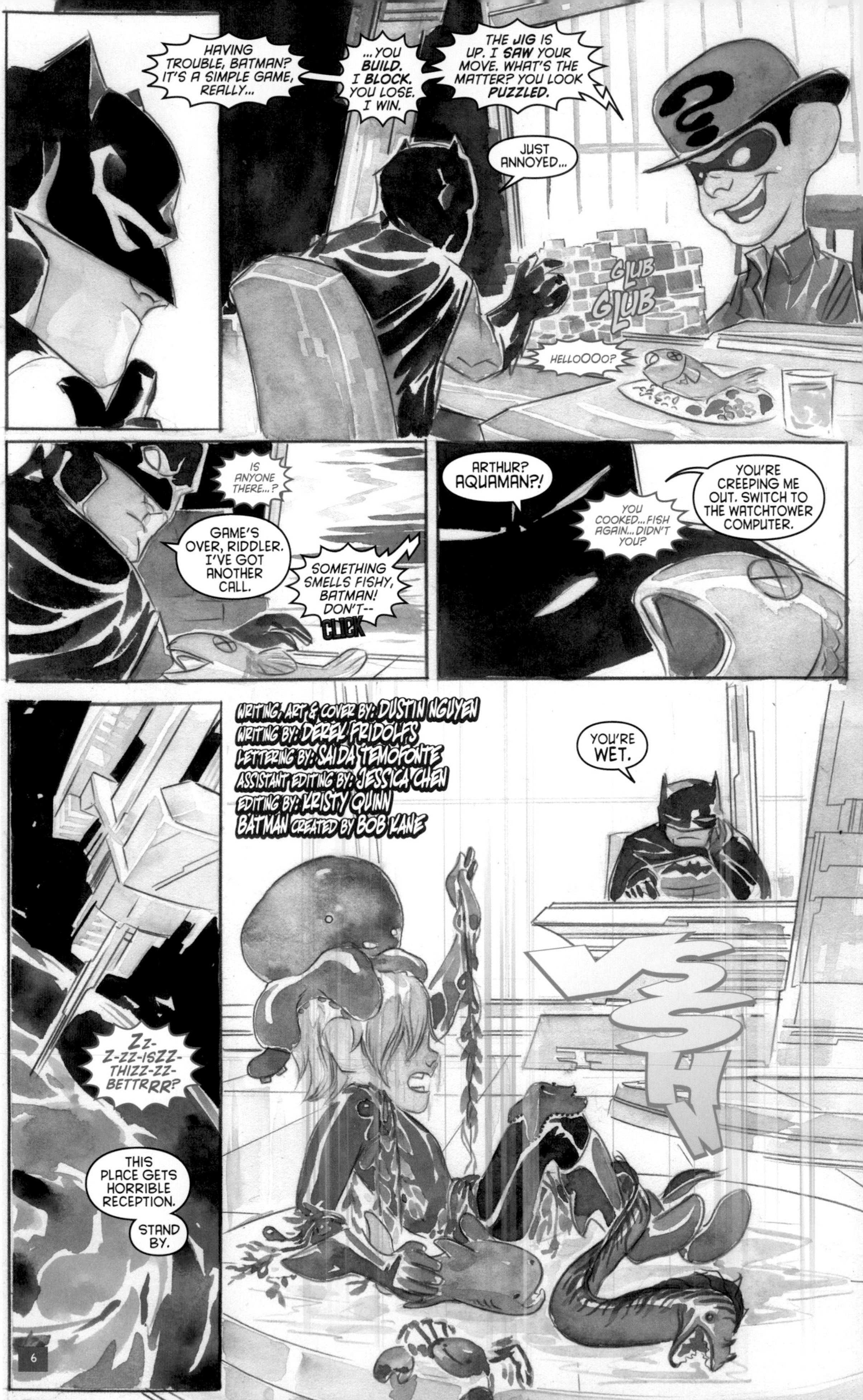
HAVING TROUBLE, BATMAN? IT'S A SIMPLE GAME, REALLY...
...YOU BUILD. I BLOCK. YOU LOSE. I WIN.
THE JIG IS UP. I SAW YOUR MOVE. WHAT'S THE MATTER? YOU LOOK PUZZLED.
JUST ANNOYED...
GLUB GLUB
HELLOOOO?
IS ANYONE THERE...?
GAME'S OVER, RIDDLER. I'VE GOT ANOTHER CALL.
SOMETHING SMELLS FISHY, BATMAN! DON'T--
CLICK
ARTHUR? AQUAMAN?!
YOU COOKED...FISH AGAIN...DIDN'T YOU?
YOU'RE CREEPING ME OUT. SWITCH TO THE WATCHTOWER COMPUTER.
WRITING, ART & COVER BY: DUSTIN NGUYEN
WRITING BY: DEREK FRIDOLFS
LETTERING BY: SAIDA TEMOFONTE
ASSISTANT EDITING BY: JESSICA CHEN
EDITING BY: KRISTY QUINN
BATMAN CREATED BY BOB KANE
YOU'RE WET.
ZZ-Z-ZZ-ISZZ-THIZZ-ZZ-BETTRRR?
THIS PLACE GETS HORRIBLE RECEPTION.
STAND BY.

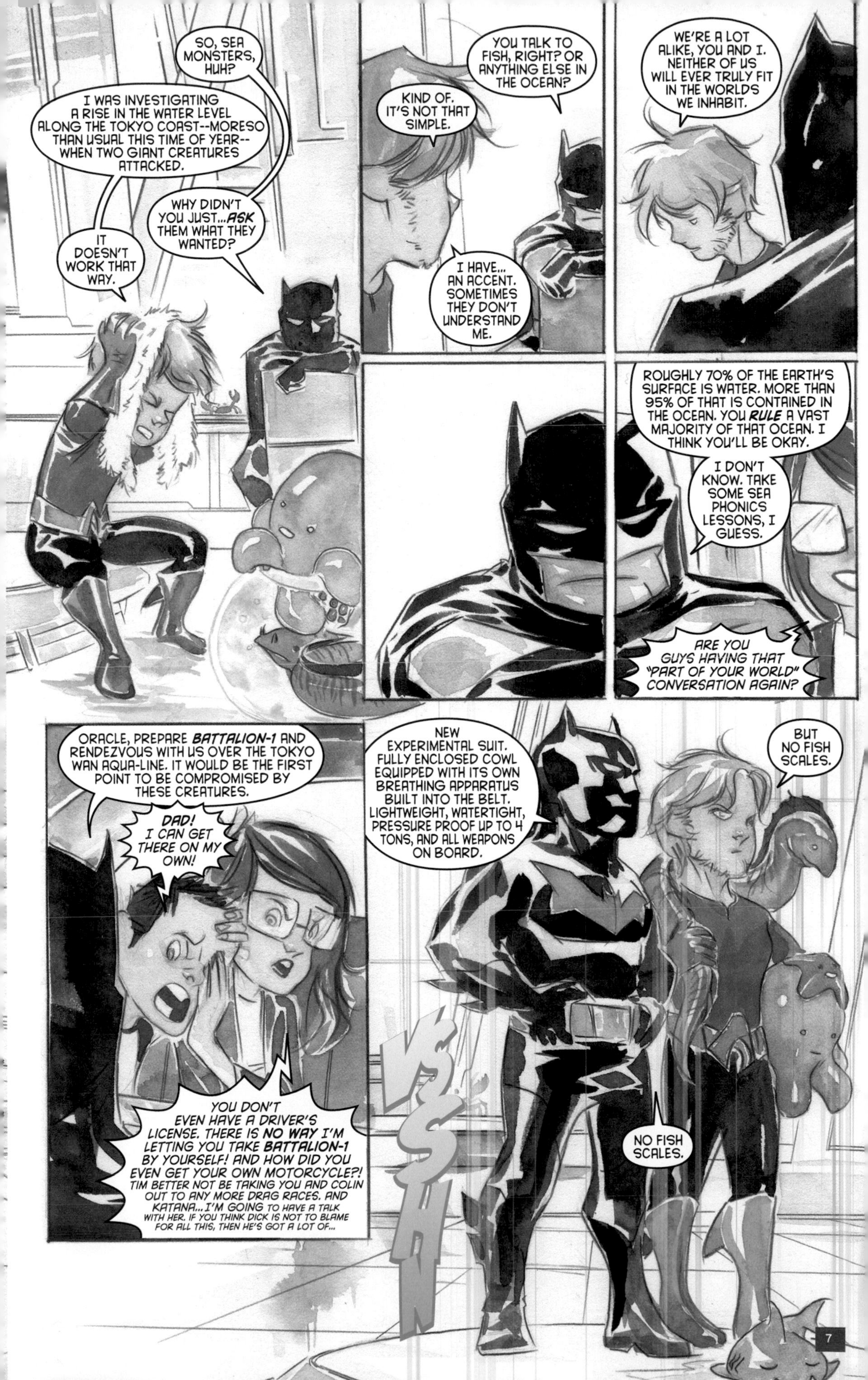

I WAS INVESTIGATING A RISE IN THE WATER LEVEL ALONG THE TOKYO COAST--MORESO THAN USUAL THIS TIME OF YEAR-- WHEN TWO GIANT CREATURES ATTACKED.
SO, SEA MONSTERS, HUH?
IT DOESN'T WORK THAT WAY.
WHY DIDN'T YOU JUST...ASK THEM WHAT THEY WANTED?
YOU TALK TO FISH, RIGHT? OR ANYTHING ELSE IN THE OCEAN?
KIND OF. IT'S NOT THAT SIMPLE.
I HAVE... AN ACCENT. SOMETIMES THEY DON'T UNDERSTAND ME.
WE'RE A LOT ALIKE, YOU AND I. NEITHER OF US WILL EVER TRULY FIT IN THE WORLDS WE INHABIT.
ROUGHLY 70% OF THE EARTH'S SURFACE IS WATER. MORE THAN 95% OF THAT IS CONTAINED IN THE OCEAN. YOU RULE A VAST MAJORITY OF THAT OCEAN. I THINK YOU'LL BE OKAY.
I DON'T KNOW. TAKE SOME SEA PHONICS LESSONS, I GUESS.
ARE YOU GUYS HAVING THAT "PART OF YOUR WORLD" CONVERSATION AGAIN?
ORACLE, PREPARE BATTALION-1 AND RENDEZVOUS WITH US OVER THE TOKYO WAN AQUA-LINE. IT WOULD BE THE FIRST POINT TO BE COMPROMISED BY THESE CREATURES.
DAD! I CAN GET THERE ON MY OWN!
YOU DON'T EVEN HAVE A DRIVER'S LICENSE. THERE IS NO WAY I'M LETTING YOU TAKE BATTALION-1 BY YOURSELF! AND HOW DID YOU EVEN GET YOUR OWN MOTORCYCLE?! TIM BETTER NOT BE TAKING YOU AND COLIN OUT TO ANY MORE DRAG RACES. AND KATANA...I'M GOING TO HAVE A TALK WITH HER. IF YOU THINK DICK IS NOT TO BLAME FOR ALL THIS, THEN HE'S GOT A LOT OF...
NEW EXPERIMENTAL SUIT. FULLY ENCLOSED COWL EQUIPPED WITH ITS OWN BREATHING APPARATUS BUILT INTO THE BELT. LIGHTWEIGHT, WATERTIGHT, PRESSURE PROOF UP TO 4 TONS, AND ALL WEAPONS ON BOARD.
BUT NO FISH SCALES.
NO FISH SCALES.
VSSH

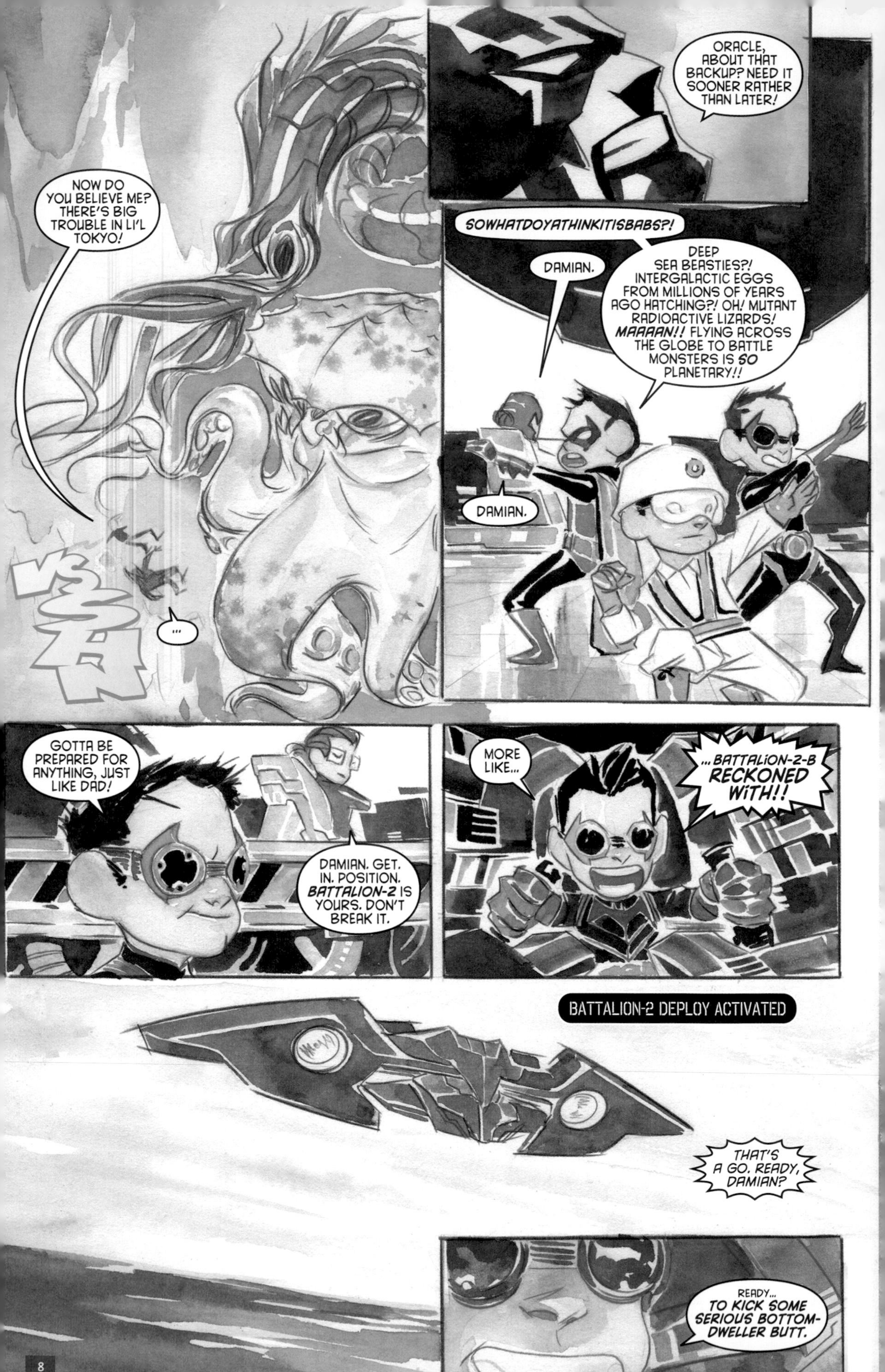

ORACLE, ABOUT THAT BACKUP? NEED IT SOONER RATHER THAN LATER!
NOW DO YOU BELIEVE ME? THERE'S BIG TROUBLE IN LI'L TOKYO!
...
SOWHATDOYATHINKITISBABS?!
DAMIAN.
DEEP SEA BEASTIES?! INTERGALACTIC EGGS FROM MILLIONS OF YEARS AGO HATCHING?! OH! MUTANT RADIOACTIVE LIZARDS! MAAAAN!! FLYING ACROSS THE GLOBE TO BATTLE MONSTERS IS SO PLANETARY!!
DAMIAN.
GOTTA BE PREPARED FOR ANYTHING, JUST LIKE DAD!
DAMIAN. GET. IN. POSITION. BATTALION-2 IS YOURS. DON'T BREAK IT.
MORE LIKE...
...BATTALION-2-B RECKONED WITH!!
BATTALION-2 DEPLOY ACTIVATED
THAT'S A GO. READY, DAMIAN?
READY... TO KICK SOME SERIOUS BOTTOM-DWELLER BUTT.

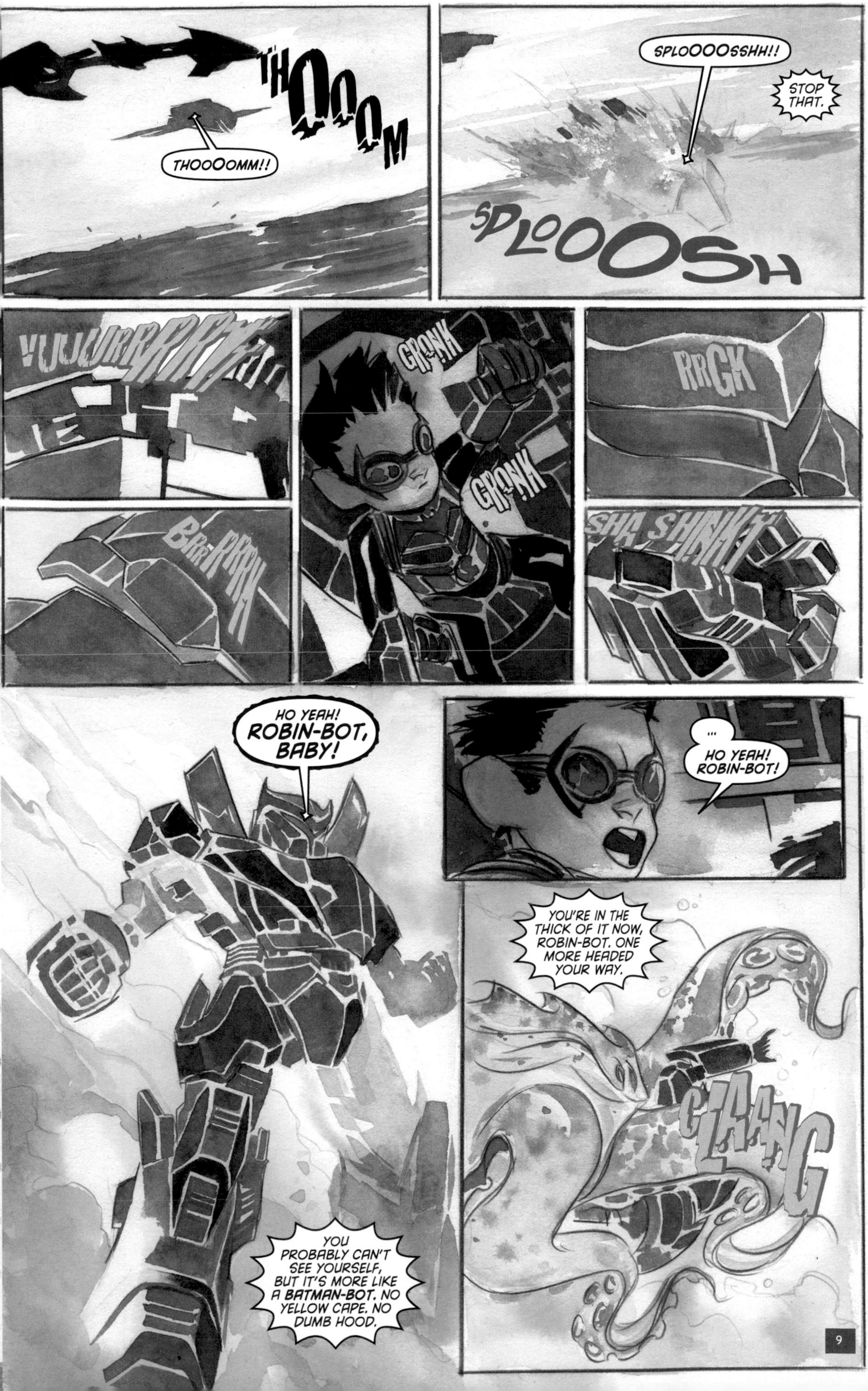
THOOOM
THOOOOMM!!
SPLOOOOSSHH!!
STOP THAT.
SPLOOOSH
VUUURRRRRT
GRONK
GRONK
RRGK
BRRRRRK
SHA SHINK
HO YEAH! ROBIN-BOT, BABY!
... HO YEAH! ROBIN-BOT!
YOU'RE IN THE THICK OF IT NOW, ROBIN-BOT. ONE MORE HEADED YOUR WAY.
CLAANG
YOU PROBABLY CAN'T SEE YOURSELF, BUT IT'S MORE LIKE A BATMAN-BOT. NO YELLOW CAPE. NO DUMB HOOD.

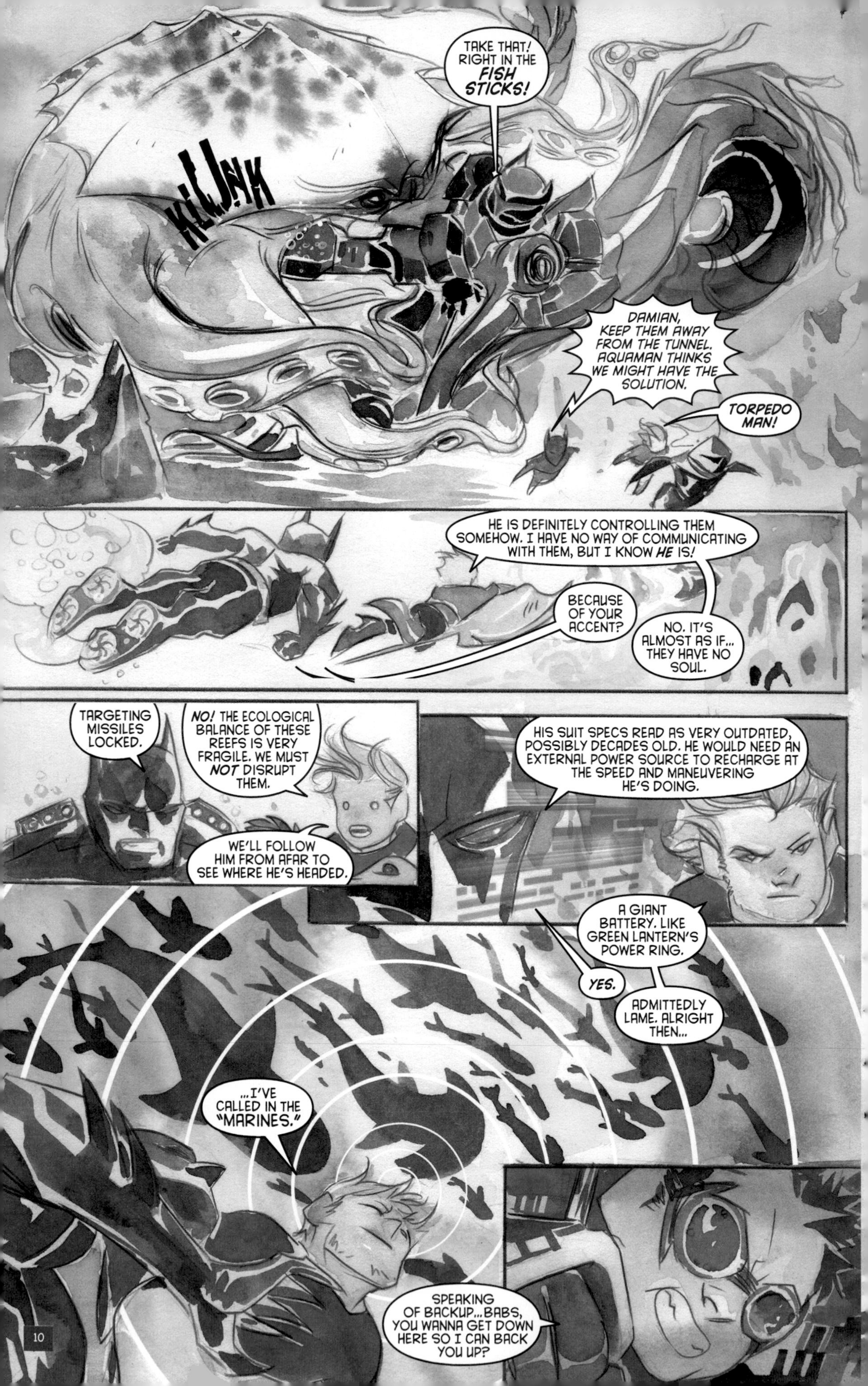
TAKE THAT! RIGHT IN THE FISH STICKS!
KLUNK
DAMIAN, KEEP THEM AWAY FROM THE TUNNEL. AQUAMAN THINKS WE MIGHT HAVE THE SOLUTION.
TORPEDO MAN!
HE IS DEFINITELY CONTROLLING THEM SOMEHOW. I HAVE NO WAY OF COMMUNICATING WITH THEM, BUT I KNOW HE IS!
BECAUSE OF YOUR ACCENT?
NO. IT'S ALMOST AS IF... THEY HAVE NO SOUL.
TARGETING MISSILES LOCKED.
NO! THE ECOLOGICAL BALANCE OF THESE REEFS IS VERY FRAGILE. WE MUST NOT DISRUPT THEM.
WE'LL FOLLOW HIM FROM AFAR TO SEE WHERE HE'S HEADED.
HIS SUIT SPECS READ AS VERY OUTDATED, POSSIBLY DECADES OLD. HE WOULD NEED AN EXTERNAL POWER SOURCE TO RECHARGE AT THE SPEED AND MANEUVERING HE'S DOING.
A GIANT BATTERY. LIKE GREEN LANTERN'S POWER RING.
YES.
ADMITTEDLY LAME. ALRIGHT THEN...
...I'VE CALLED IN THE "MARINES."
SPEAKING OF BACKUP... BABS, YOU WANNA GET DOWN HERE SO I CAN BACK YOU UP?

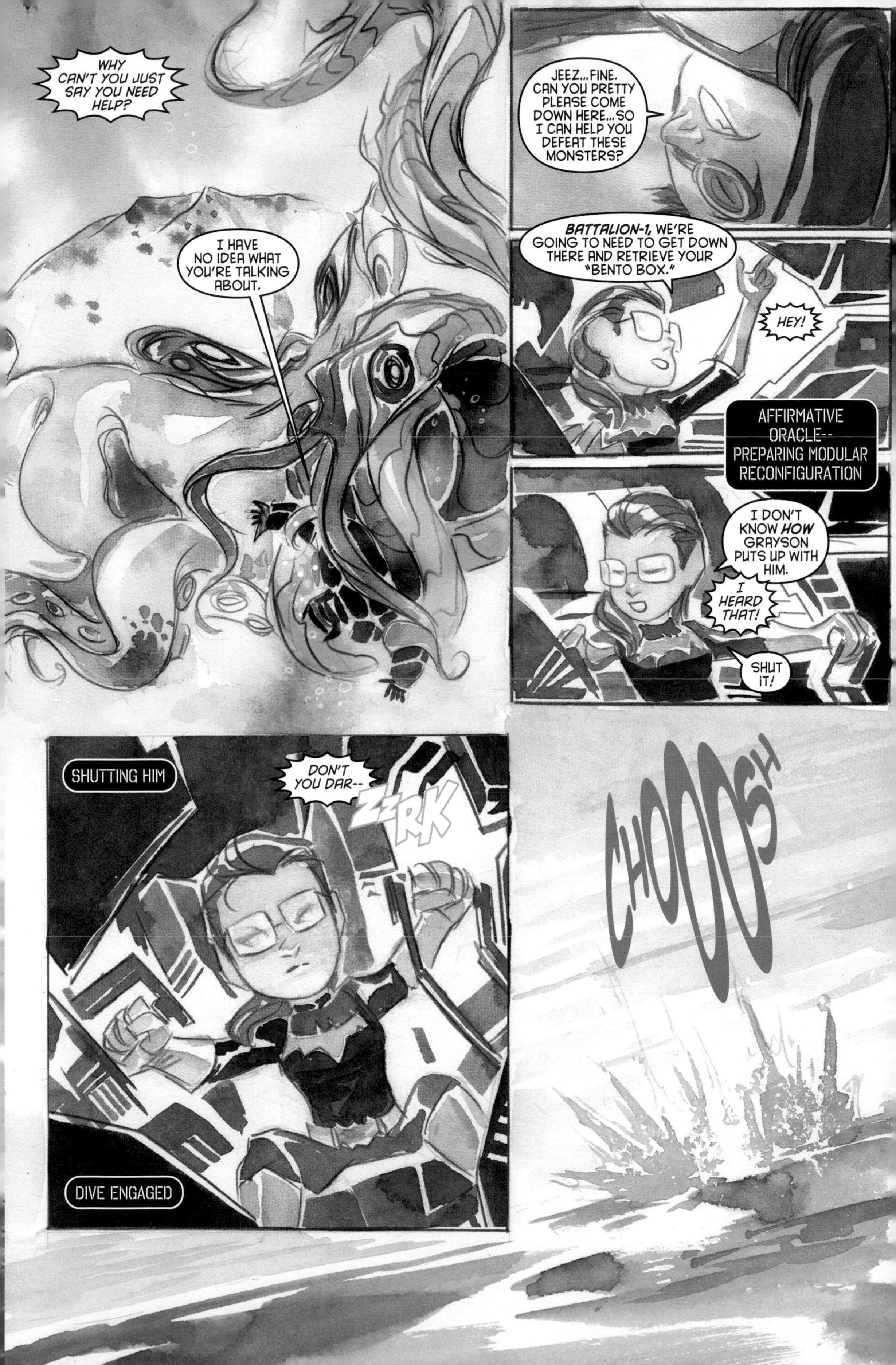
WHY CAN'T YOU JUST SAY YOU NEED HELP?
I HAVE NO IDEA WHAT YOU'RE TALKING ABOUT.
JEEZ...FINE. CAN YOU PRETTY PLEASE COME DOWN HERE...SO I CAN HELP YOU DEFEAT THESE MONSTERS?
BATTALION-1, WE'RE GOING TO NEED TO GET DOWN THERE AND RETRIEVE YOUR "BENTO BOX."
HEY!
AFFIRMATIVE ORACLE-- PREPARING MODULAR RECONFIGURATION
I DON'T KNOW HOW GRAYSON PUTS UP WITH HIM.
I HEARD THAT!
SHUT IT!
SHUTTING HIM
DON'T YOU DAR--
ZZRK
DIVE ENGAGED
CHOOOSH

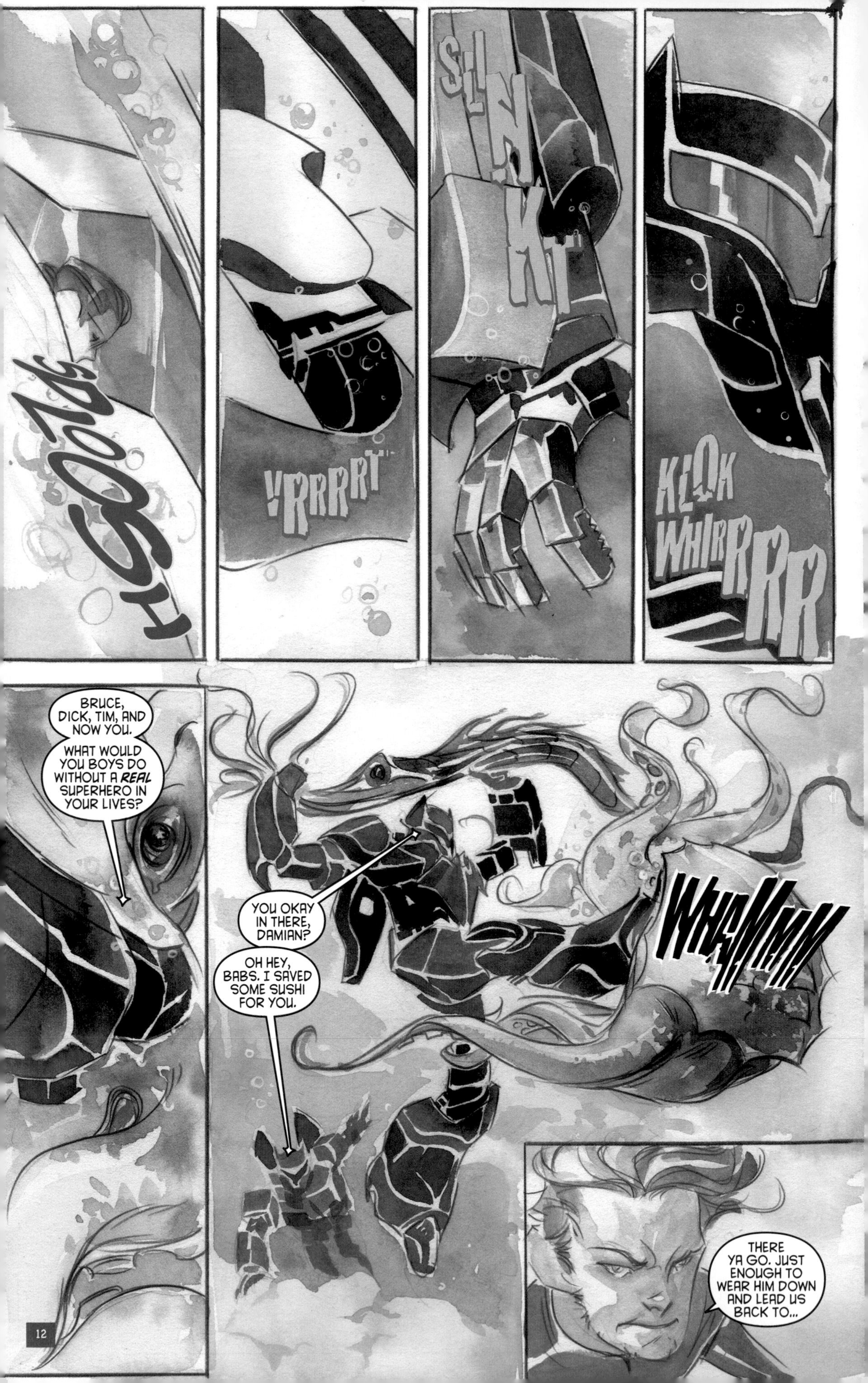

HSPLOOSH
VRRRRT
SHNKT
KLOK
WHIRRRRR
BRUCE, DICK, TIM, AND NOW YOU.
WHAT WOULD YOU BOYS DO WITHOUT A *REAL* SUPERHERO IN YOUR LIVES?
YOU OKAY IN THERE, DAMIAN?
OH HEY, BABS. I SAVED SOME SUSHI FOR YOU.
WHAMMM
THERE YA GO. JUST ENOUGH TO WEAR HIM DOWN AND LEAD US BACK TO...

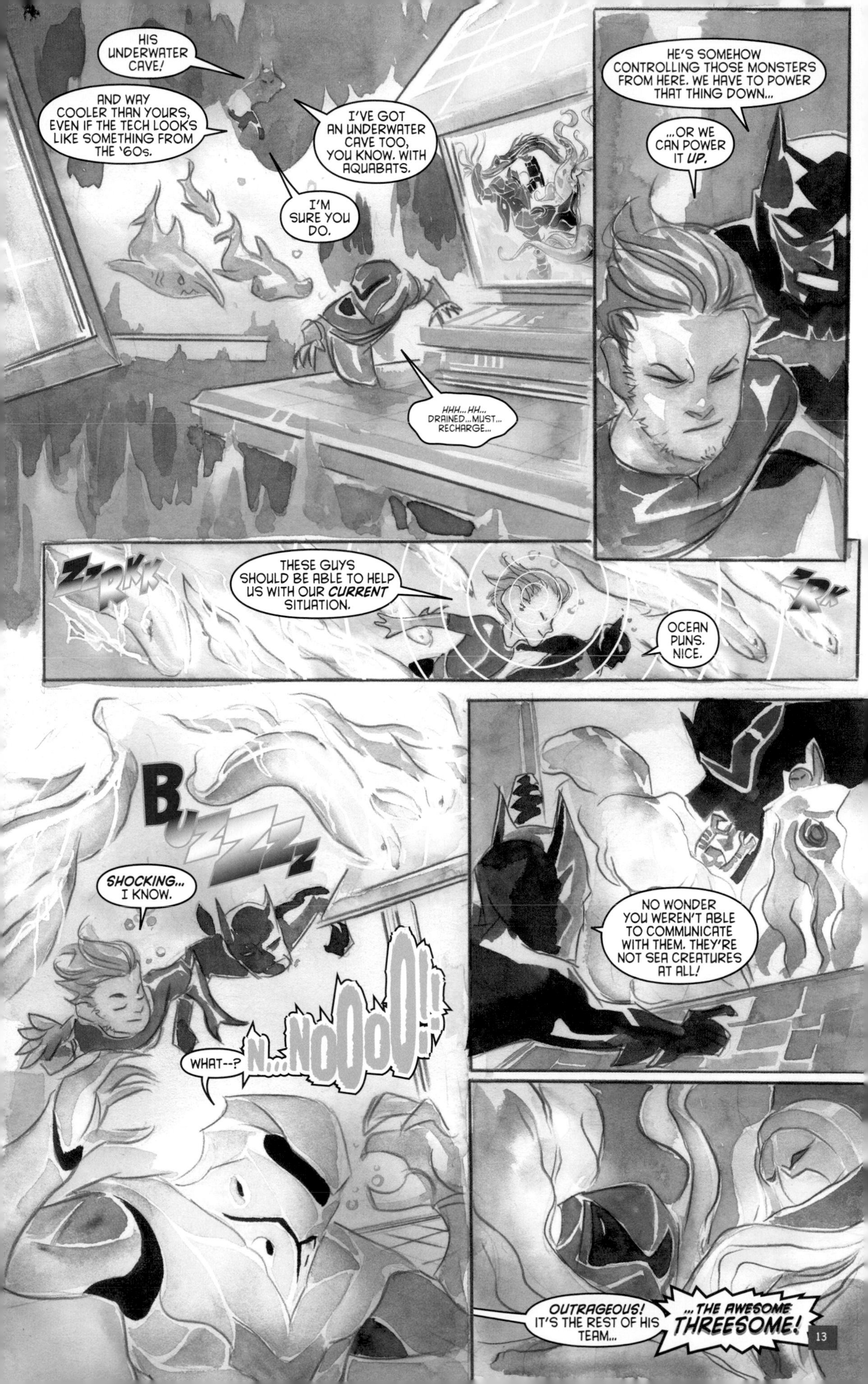
HIS UNDERWATER CAVE!
AND WAY COOLER THAN YOURS, EVEN IF THE TECH LOOKS LIKE SOMETHING FROM THE '60s.
I'VE GOT AN UNDERWATER CAVE TOO, YOU KNOW. WITH AQUABATS.
I'M SURE YOU DO.
HHH...HH... DRAINED...MUST... RECHARGE...
HE'S SOMEHOW CONTROLLING THOSE MONSTERS FROM HERE. WE HAVE TO POWER THAT THING DOWN...
...OR WE CAN POWER IT UP.
ZZRKK
THESE GUYS SHOULD BE ABLE TO HELP US WITH OUR CURRENT SITUATION.
ZRK
OCEAN PUNS. NICE.
BUZZZZ
SHOCKING... I KNOW.
WHAT--?
N...NOOOO!!
NO WONDER YOU WEREN'T ABLE TO COMMUNICATE WITH THEM. THEY'RE NOT SEA CREATURES AT ALL!
OUTRAGEOUS! IT'S THE REST OF HIS TEAM...
...THE AWESOME THREESOME!

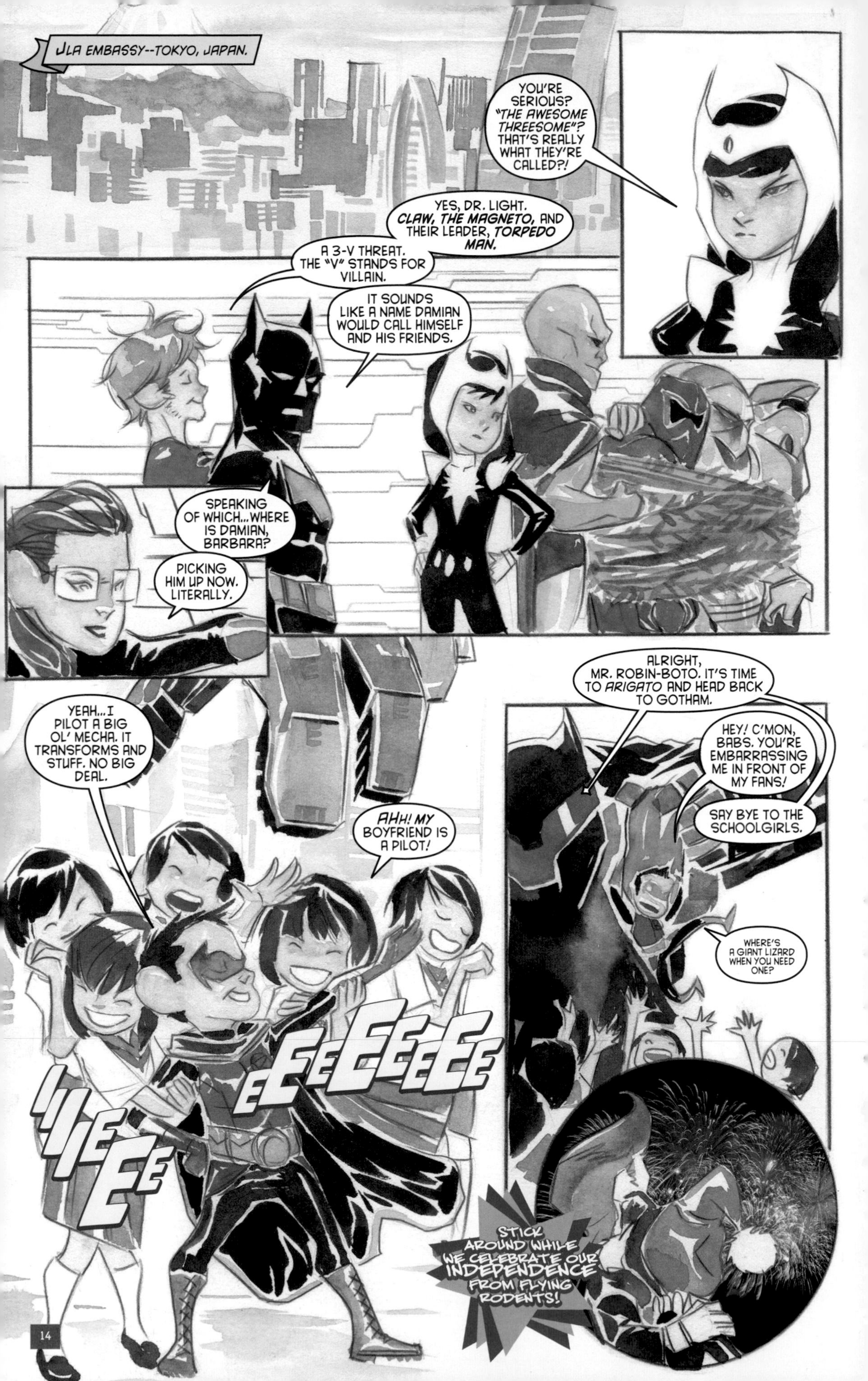
JLA EMBASSY--TOKYO, JAPAN.
YOU'RE SERIOUS? "THE AWESOME THREESOME"? THAT'S REALLY WHAT THEY'RE CALLED?!
YES, DR. LIGHT. CLAW, THE MAGNETO, AND THEIR LEADER, TORPEDO MAN.
A 3-V THREAT. THE "V" STANDS FOR VILLAIN.
IT SOUNDS LIKE A NAME DAMIAN WOULD CALL HIMSELF AND HIS FRIENDS.
SPEAKING OF WHICH...WHERE IS DAMIAN, BARBARA?
PICKING HIM UP NOW. LITERALLY.
YEAH...I PILOT A BIG OL' MECHA. IT TRANSFORMS AND STUFF. NO BIG DEAL.
AHH! MY BOYFRIEND IS A PILOT!
IIIIEEE
EEEEEEEEE
ALRIGHT, MR. ROBIN-BOTO. IT'S TIME TO ARIGATO AND HEAD BACK TO GOTHAM.
HEY! C'MON, BABS. YOU'RE EMBARRASSING ME IN FRONT OF MY FANS!
SAY BYE TO THE SCHOOLGIRLS.
WHERE'S A GIANT LIZARD WHEN YOU NEED ONE?
STICK AROUND WHILE WE CELEBRATE OUR INDEPENDENCE FROM FLYING RODENTS!

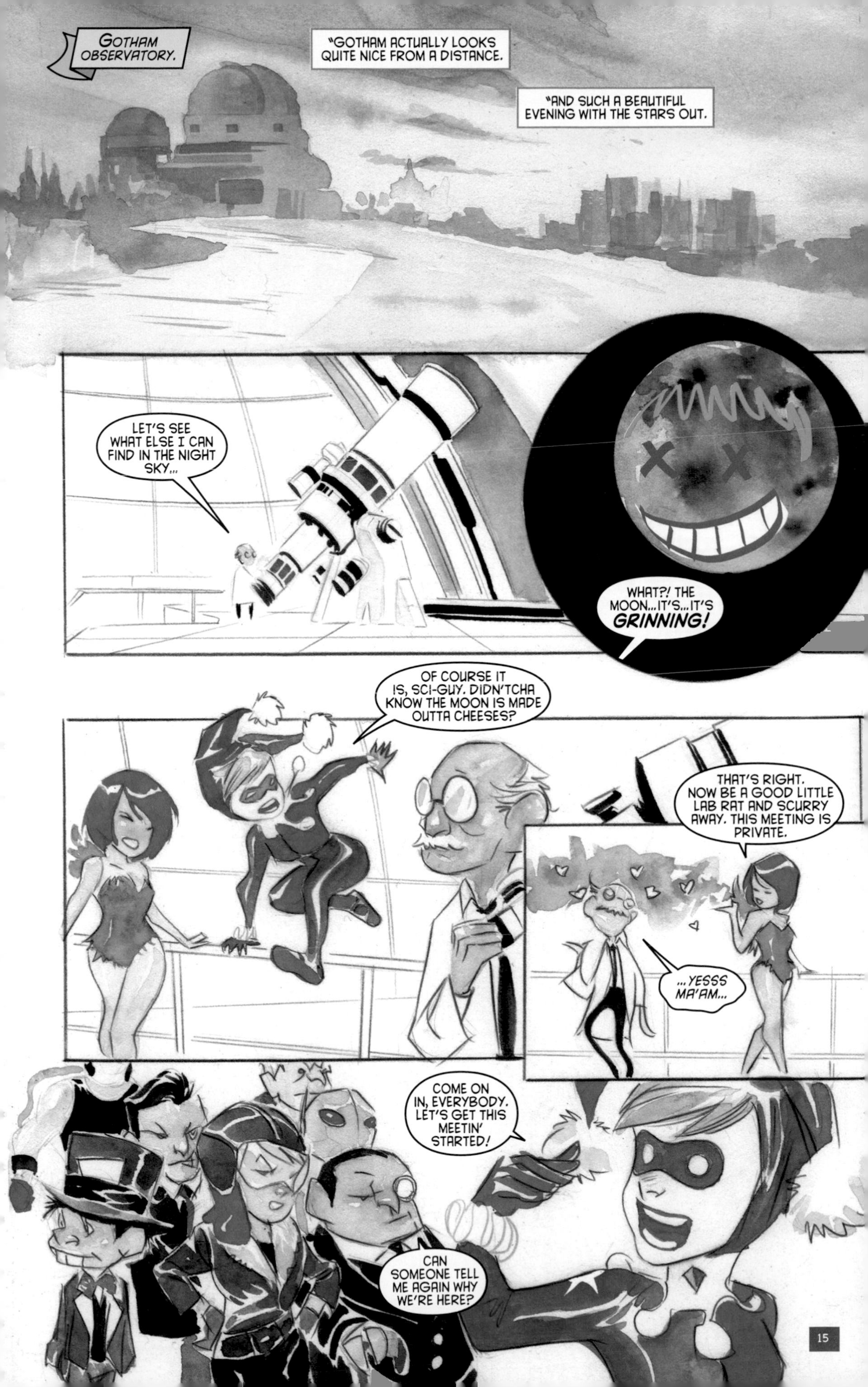
GOTHAM OBSERVATORY.
"GOTHAM ACTUALLY LOOKS QUITE NICE FROM A DISTANCE.
"AND SUCH A BEAUTIFUL EVENING WITH THE STARS OUT.
LET'S SEE WHAT ELSE I CAN FIND IN THE NIGHT SKY...
WHAT?! THE MOON...IT'S...IT'S GRINNING!
OF COURSE IT IS, SCI-GUY. DIDN'TCHA KNOW THE MOON IS MADE OUTTA CHEESES?
THAT'S RIGHT. NOW BE A GOOD LITTLE LAB RAT AND SCURRY AWAY. THIS MEETING IS PRIVATE.
...YESSS MA'AM...
COME ON IN, EVERYBODY. LET'S GET THIS MEETIN' STARTED!
CAN SOMEONE TELL ME AGAIN WHY WE'RE HERE?

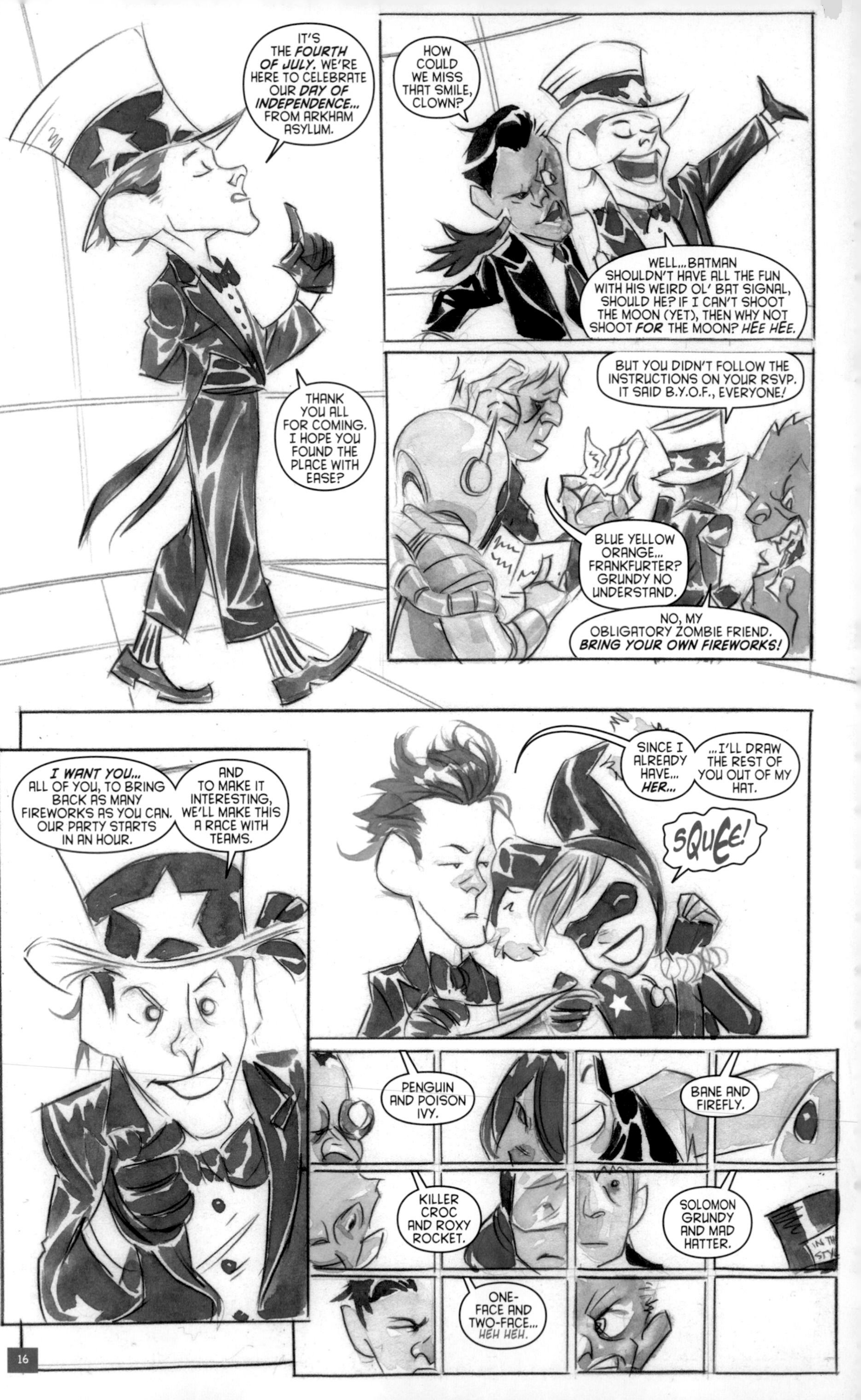

IT'S THE *FOURTH OF JULY.* WE'RE HERE TO CELEBRATE OUR *DAY OF INDEPENDENCE...* FROM ARKHAM ASYLUM.
THANK YOU ALL FOR COMING. I HOPE YOU FOUND THE PLACE WITH EASE?
HOW COULD WE MISS THAT SMILE, CLOWN?
WELL...BATMAN SHOULDN'T HAVE ALL THE FUN WITH HIS WEIRD OL' BAT SIGNAL, SHOULD HE? IF I CAN'T SHOOT THE MOON (YET), THEN WHY NOT SHOOT *FOR* THE MOON? *HEE HEE.*
BUT YOU DIDN'T FOLLOW THE INSTRUCTIONS ON YOUR RSVP. IT SAID B.Y.O.F., EVERYONE!
BLUE YELLOW ORANGE... FRANKFURTER? GRUNDY NO UNDERSTAND.
NO, MY OBLIGATORY ZOMBIE FRIEND. ***BRING YOUR OWN FIREWORKS!***
I WANT YOU... ALL OF YOU, TO BRING BACK AS MANY FIREWORKS AS YOU CAN. OUR PARTY STARTS IN AN HOUR.
AND TO MAKE IT INTERESTING, WE'LL MAKE THIS A RACE WITH TEAMS.
SINCE I ALREADY HAVE... *HER...*
...I'LL DRAW THE REST OF YOU OUT OF MY HAT.
SQUEE!
PENGUIN AND POISON IVY.
BANE AND FIREFLY.
KILLER CROC AND ROXY ROCKET.
SOLOMON GRUNDY AND MAD HATTER.
ONE-FACE AND TWO-FACE... *HEH HEH.*

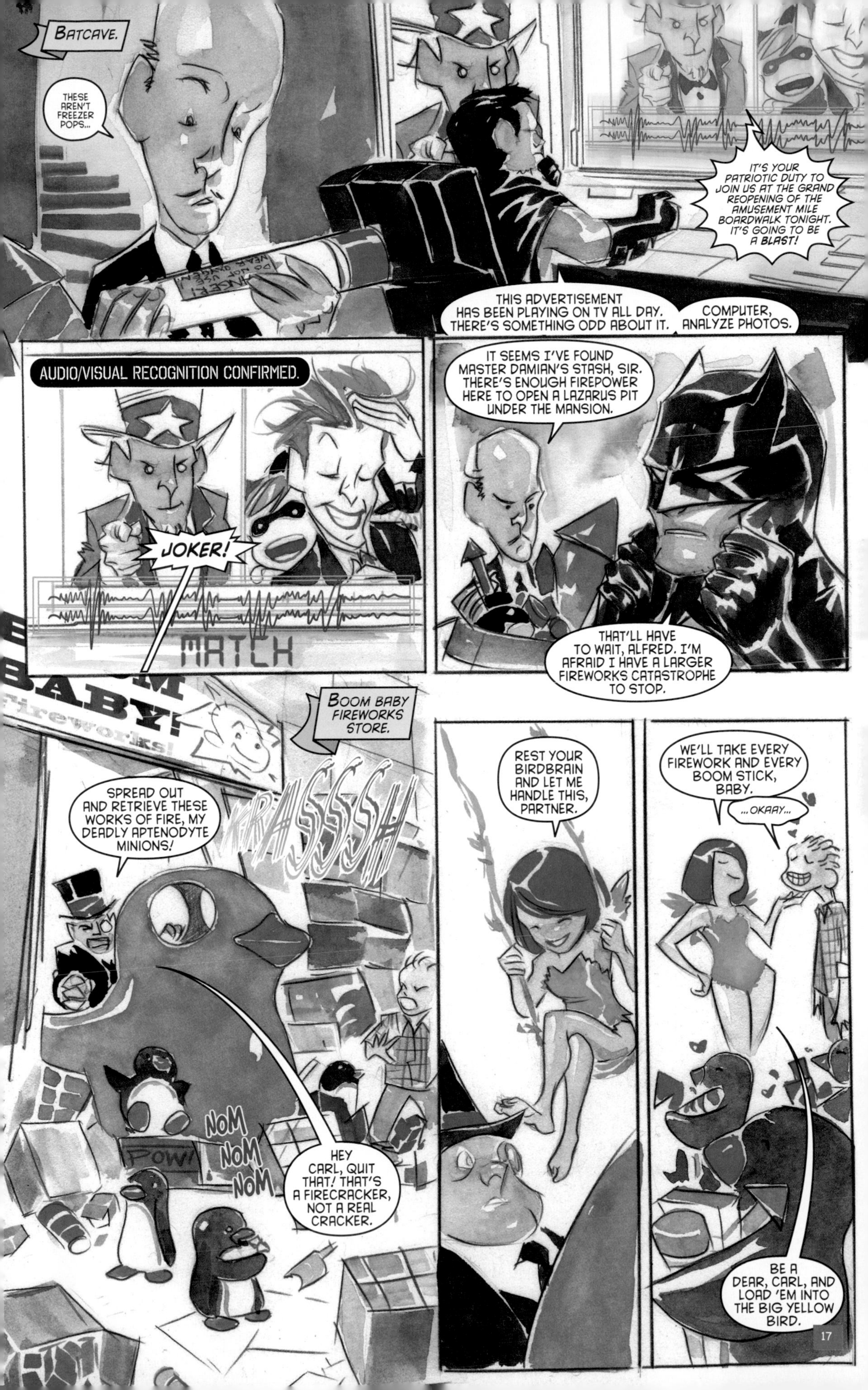

BATCAVE.
THESE AREN'T FREEZER POPS...
IT'S YOUR PATRIOTIC DUTY TO JOIN US AT THE GRAND REOPENING OF THE AMUSEMENT MILE BOARDWALK TONIGHT. IT'S GOING TO BE A BLAST!
THIS ADVERTISEMENT HAS BEEN PLAYING ON TV ALL DAY. THERE'S SOMETHING ODD ABOUT IT.
COMPUTER, ANALYZE PHOTOS.
AUDIO/VISUAL RECOGNITION CONFIRMED.
JOKER!
MATCH
IT SEEMS I'VE FOUND MASTER DAMIAN'S STASH, SIR. THERE'S ENOUGH FIREPOWER HERE TO OPEN A LAZARUS PIT UNDER THE MANSION.
THAT'LL HAVE TO WAIT, ALFRED. I'M AFRAID I HAVE A LARGER FIREWORKS CATASTROPHE TO STOP.
BOOM BABY FIREWORKS STORE.
BOOM BABY! Fireworks!
SPREAD OUT AND RETRIEVE THESE WORKS OF FIRE, MY DEADLY APTENODYTE MINIONS!
KRASSSSH
NOM NOM NOM
POW!
HEY CARL, QUIT THAT! THAT'S A FIRECRACKER, NOT A REAL CRACKER.
REST YOUR BIRDBRAIN AND LET ME HANDLE THIS, PARTNER.
WE'LL TAKE EVERY FIREWORK AND EVERY BOOM STICK, BABY.
...OKAAY...
BE A DEAR, CARL, AND LOAD 'EM INTO THE BIG YELLOW BIRD.

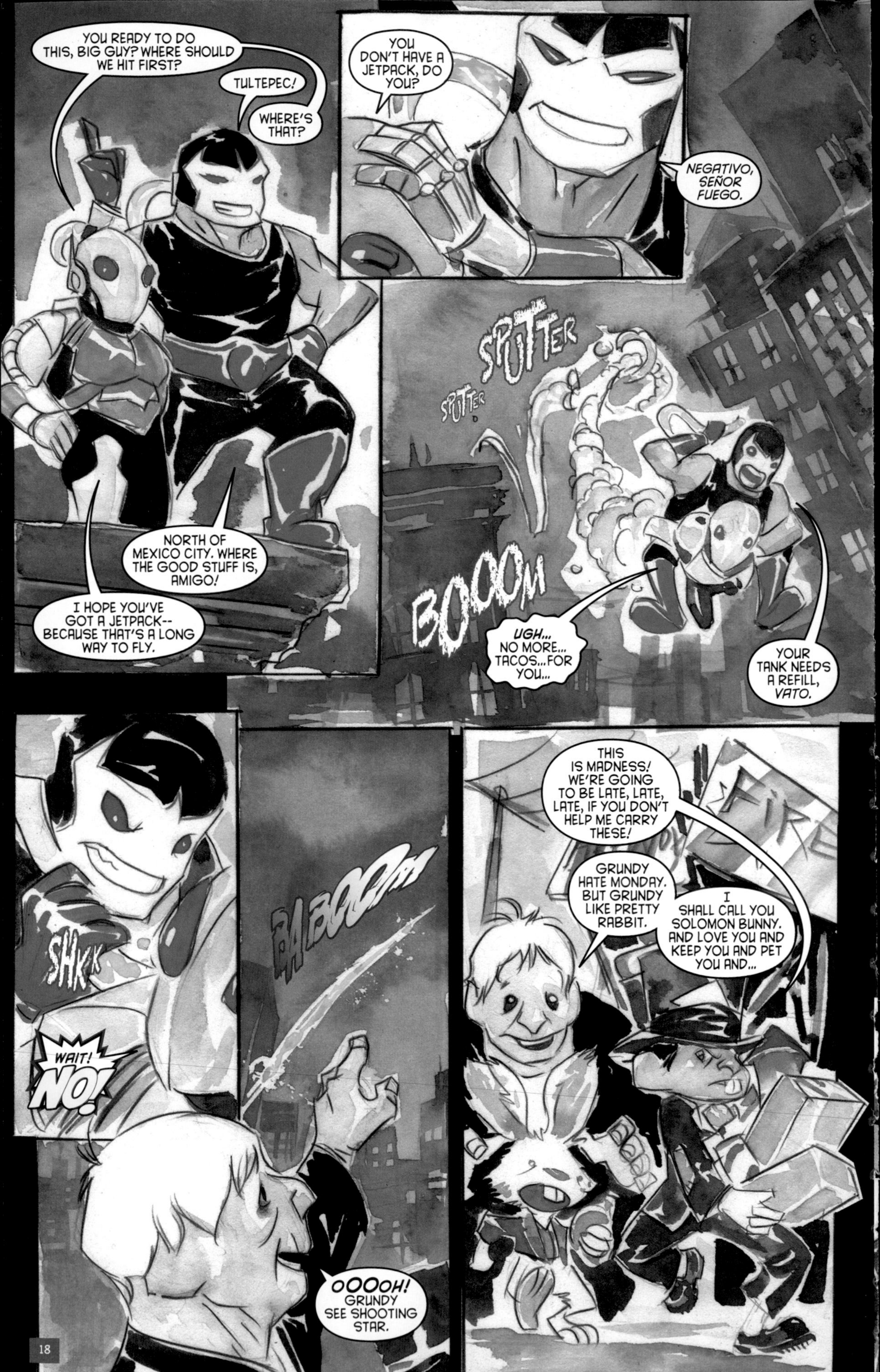
YOU READY TO DO THIS, BIG GUY? WHERE SHOULD WE HIT FIRST?
TULTEPEC!
WHERE'S THAT?
NORTH OF MEXICO CITY. WHERE THE GOOD STUFF IS, AMIGO!
I HOPE YOU'VE GOT A JETPACK-- BECAUSE THAT'S A LONG WAY TO FLY.
YOU DON'T HAVE A JETPACK, DO YOU?
NEGATIVO, SEÑOR FUEGO.
SPUTTER
SPUTTER
BOOOM
UGH... NO MORE... TACOS...FOR YOU...
YOUR TANK NEEDS A REFILL, VATO.
SHKK
WAIT! NO!
BA BOOM
OOOOH! GRUNDY SEE SHOOTING STAR.
THIS IS MADNESS! WE'RE GOING TO BE LATE, LATE, LATE, IF YOU DON'T HELP ME CARRY THESE!
FIRE
GRUNDY HATE MONDAY. BUT GRUNDY LIKE PRETTY RABBIT.
I SHALL CALL YOU SOLOMON BUNNY. AND LOVE YOU AND KEEP YOU AND PET YOU AND...

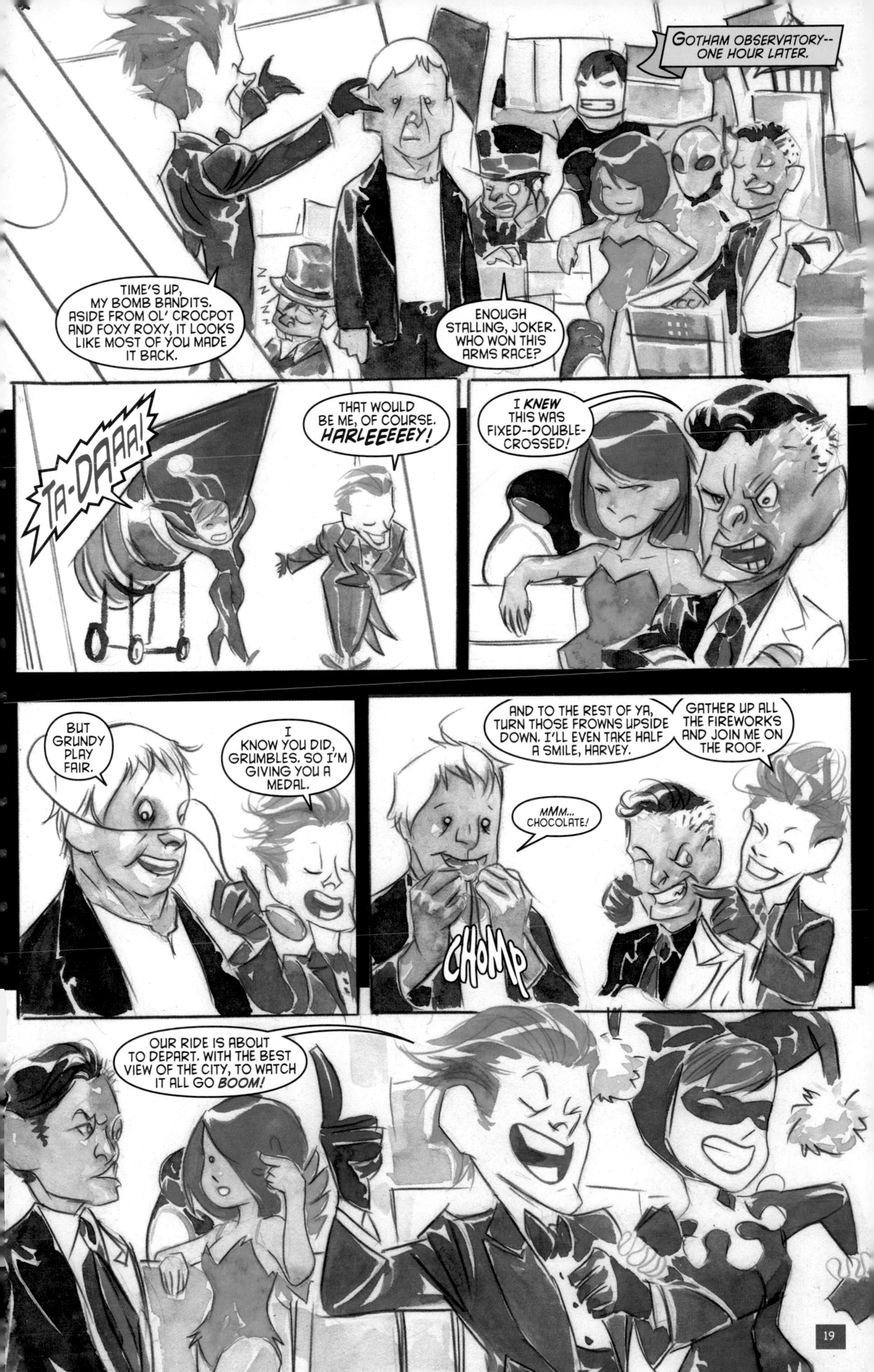

GOTHAM OBSERVATORY-- ONE HOUR LATER.
TIME'S UP, MY BOMB BANDITS. ASIDE FROM OL' CROCPOT AND FOXY ROXY, IT LOOKS LIKE MOST OF YOU MADE IT BACK.
ENOUGH STALLING, JOKER. WHO WON THIS ARMS RACE?
TA-DAAA!
THAT WOULD BE ME, OF COURSE. HARLEEEEEY!
I KNEW THIS WAS FIXED--DOUBLE-CROSSED!
BUT GRUNDY PLAY FAIR.
I KNOW YOU DID, GRUMBLES. SO I'M GIVING YOU A MEDAL.
AND TO THE REST OF YA, TURN THOSE FROWNS UPSIDE DOWN. I'LL EVEN TAKE HALF A SMILE, HARVEY.
GATHER UP ALL THE FIREWORKS AND JOIN ME ON THE ROOF.
MMM... CHOCOLATE!
CHOMP
OUR RIDE IS ABOUT TO DEPART. WITH THE BEST VIEW OF THE CITY, TO WATCH IT ALL GO BOOM!

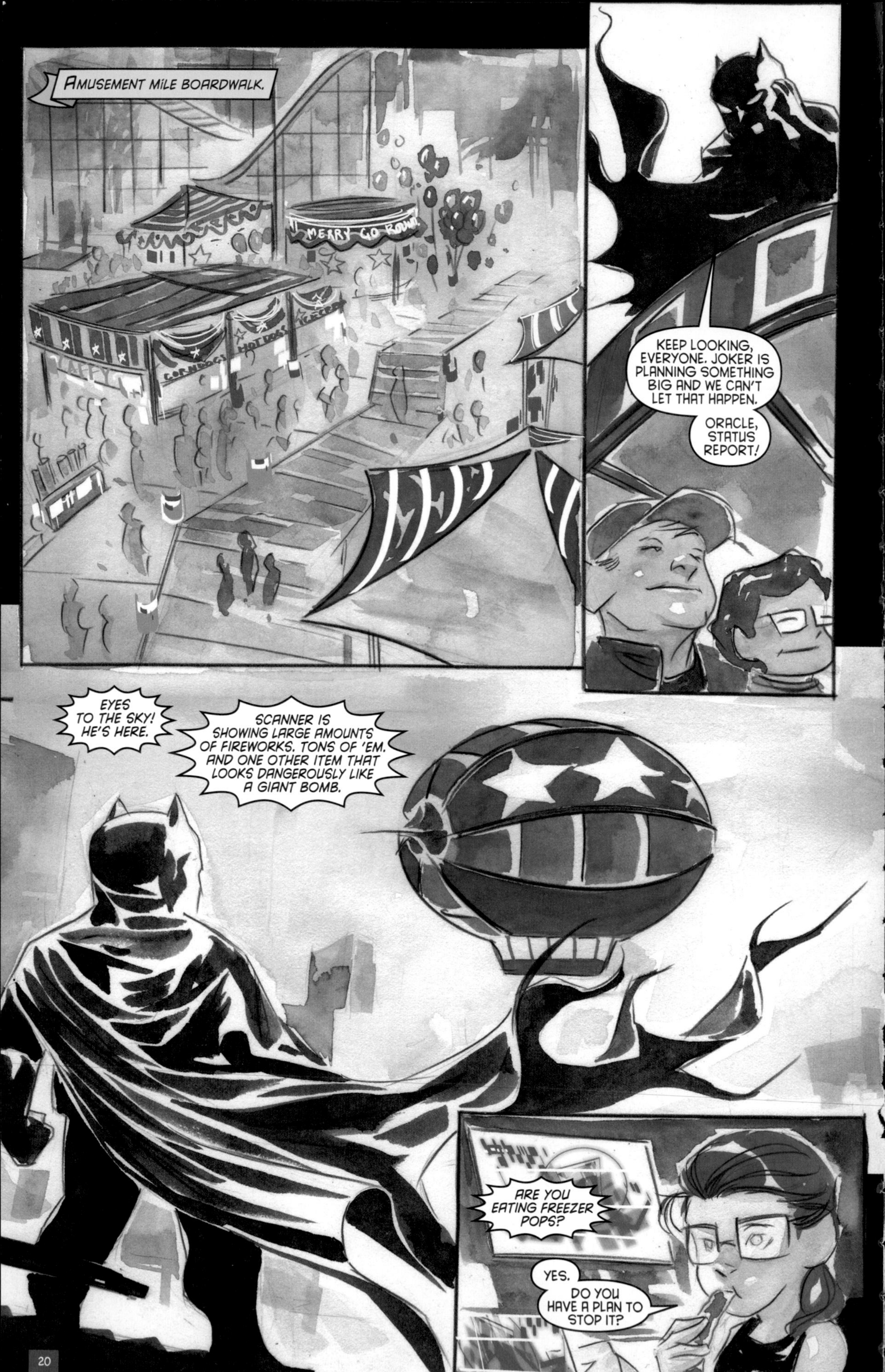
AMUSEMENT MILE BOARDWALK.
MERRY GO ROUND
CORNDOGS
HOT DOGS
KEEP LOOKING, EVERYONE. JOKER IS PLANNING SOMETHING BIG AND WE CAN'T LET THAT HAPPEN.
ORACLE, STATUS REPORT!
EYES TO THE SKY! HE'S HERE.
SCANNER IS SHOWING LARGE AMOUNTS OF FIREWORKS. TONS OF 'EM. AND ONE OTHER ITEM THAT LOOKS DANGEROUSLY LIKE A GIANT BOMB.
ARE YOU EATING FREEZER POPS?
YES.
DO YOU HAVE A PLAN TO STOP IT?

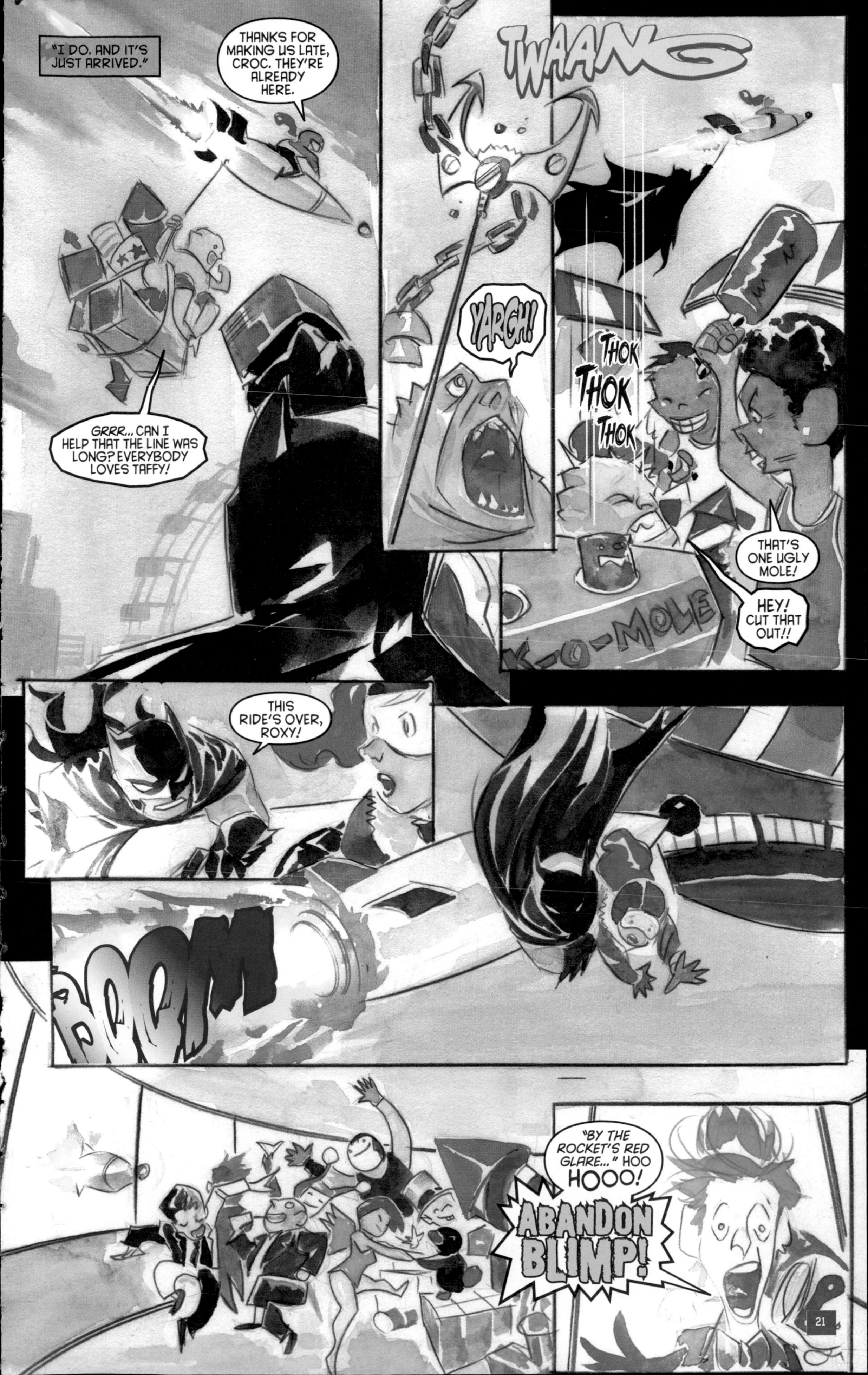

"I DO. AND IT'S JUST ARRIVED."
THANKS FOR MAKING US LATE, CROC. THEY'RE ALREADY HERE.
GRRR... CAN I HELP THAT THE LINE WAS LONG? EVERYBODY LOVES TAFFY!
TWAANG
YARGH!
THOK
THOK
THOK
THAT'S ONE UGLY MOLE!
HEY! CUT THAT OUT!!
K-O-MOLE
THIS RIDE'S OVER, ROXY!
BOOM
"BY THE ROCKET'S RED GLARE..." HOO HOOO!
ABANDON BLIMP!

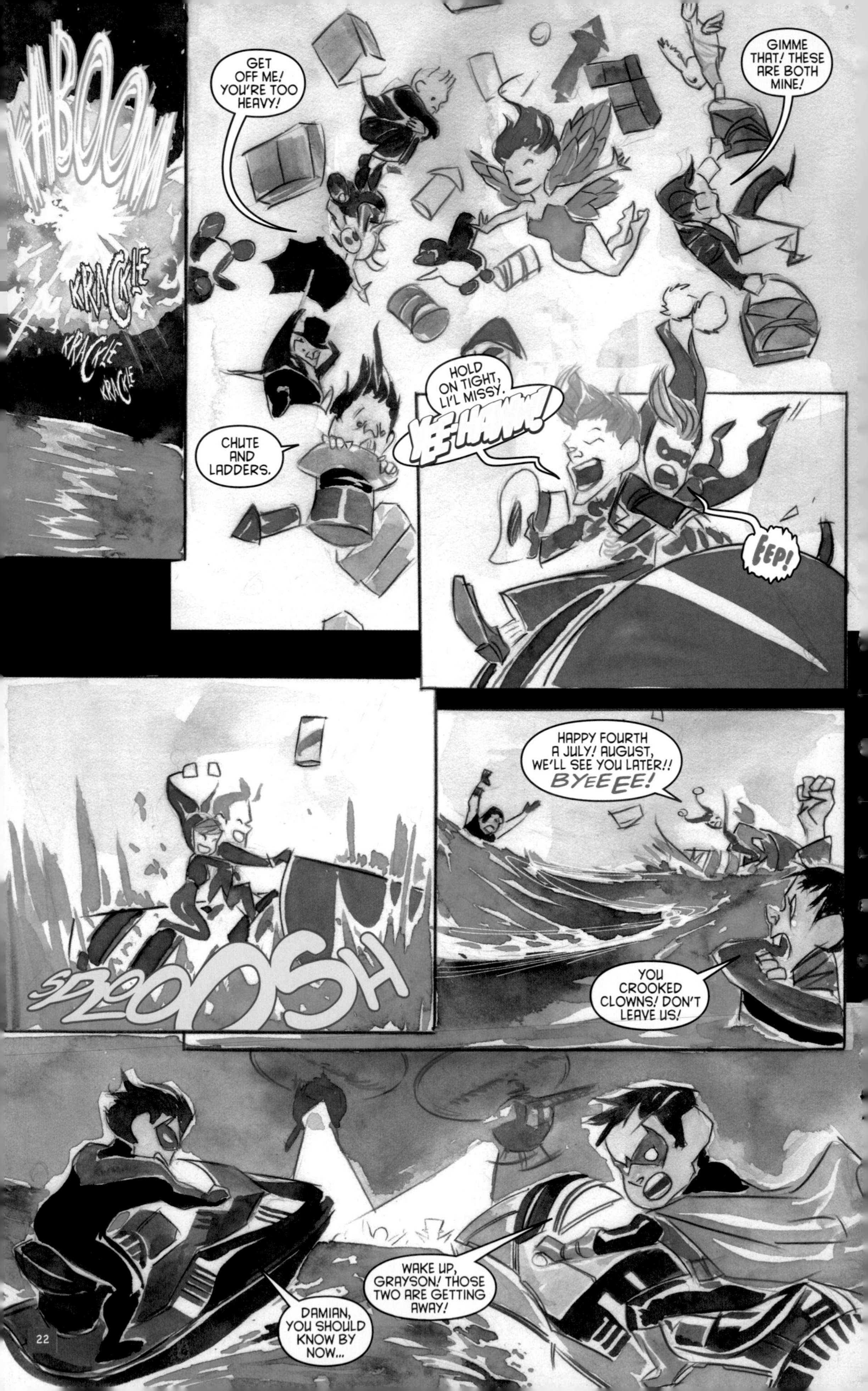

KABOOM
KRACKLE
KRACKLE
KRACKLE
GET OFF ME! YOU'RE TOO HEAVY!
GIMME THAT! THESE ARE BOTH MINE!
CHUTE AND LADDERS.
HOLD ON TIGHT, LI'L MISSY.
YEE-HAWW!
EEP!
SPLOOOSH
HAPPY FOURTH A JULY! AUGUST, WE'LL SEE YOU LATER!! BYEEEEE!
YOU CROOKED CLOWNS! DON'T LEAVE US!
WAKE UP, GRAYSON! THOSE TWO ARE GETTING AWAY!
DAMIAN, YOU SHOULD KNOW BY NOW...

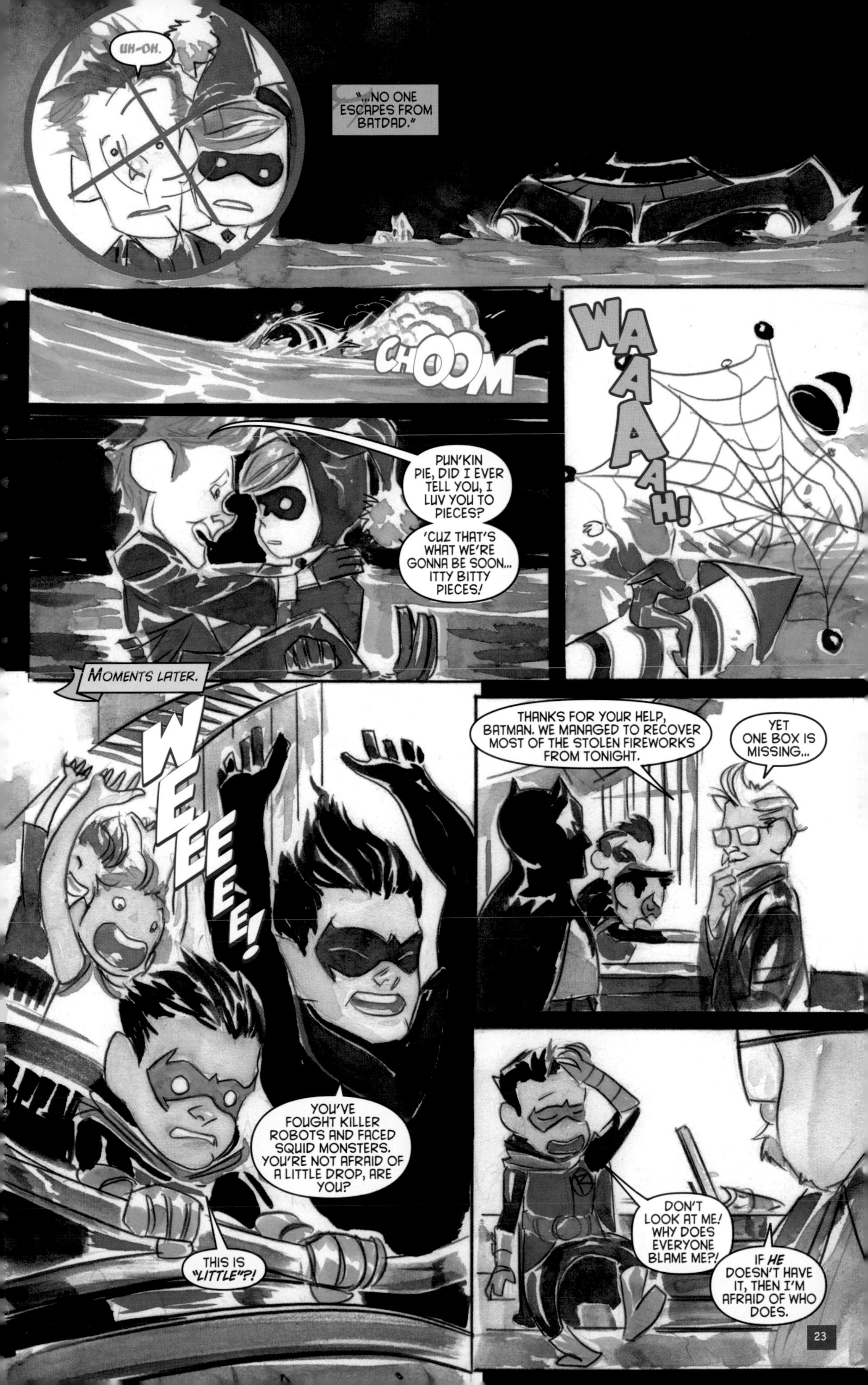
UH-OH.
"...NO ONE ESCAPES FROM BATDAD."
CHOOM
PUN'KIN PIE, DID I EVER TELL YOU, I LUV YOU TO PIECES?
'CUZ THAT'S WHAT WE'RE GONNA BE SOON... ITTY BITTY PIECES!
WAAAAAH!
MOMENTS LATER.
WEEEEEE!
YOU'VE FOUGHT KILLER ROBOTS AND FACED SQUID MONSTERS. YOU'RE NOT AFRAID OF A LITTLE DROP, ARE YOU?
THIS IS "LITTLE"?!
THANKS FOR YOUR HELP, BATMAN. WE MANAGED TO RECOVER MOST OF THE STOLEN FIREWORKS FROM TONIGHT.
YET ONE BOX IS MISSING...
DON'T LOOK AT ME! WHY DOES EVERYONE BLAME ME?!
IF HE DOESN'T HAVE IT, THEN I'M AFRAID OF WHO DOES.

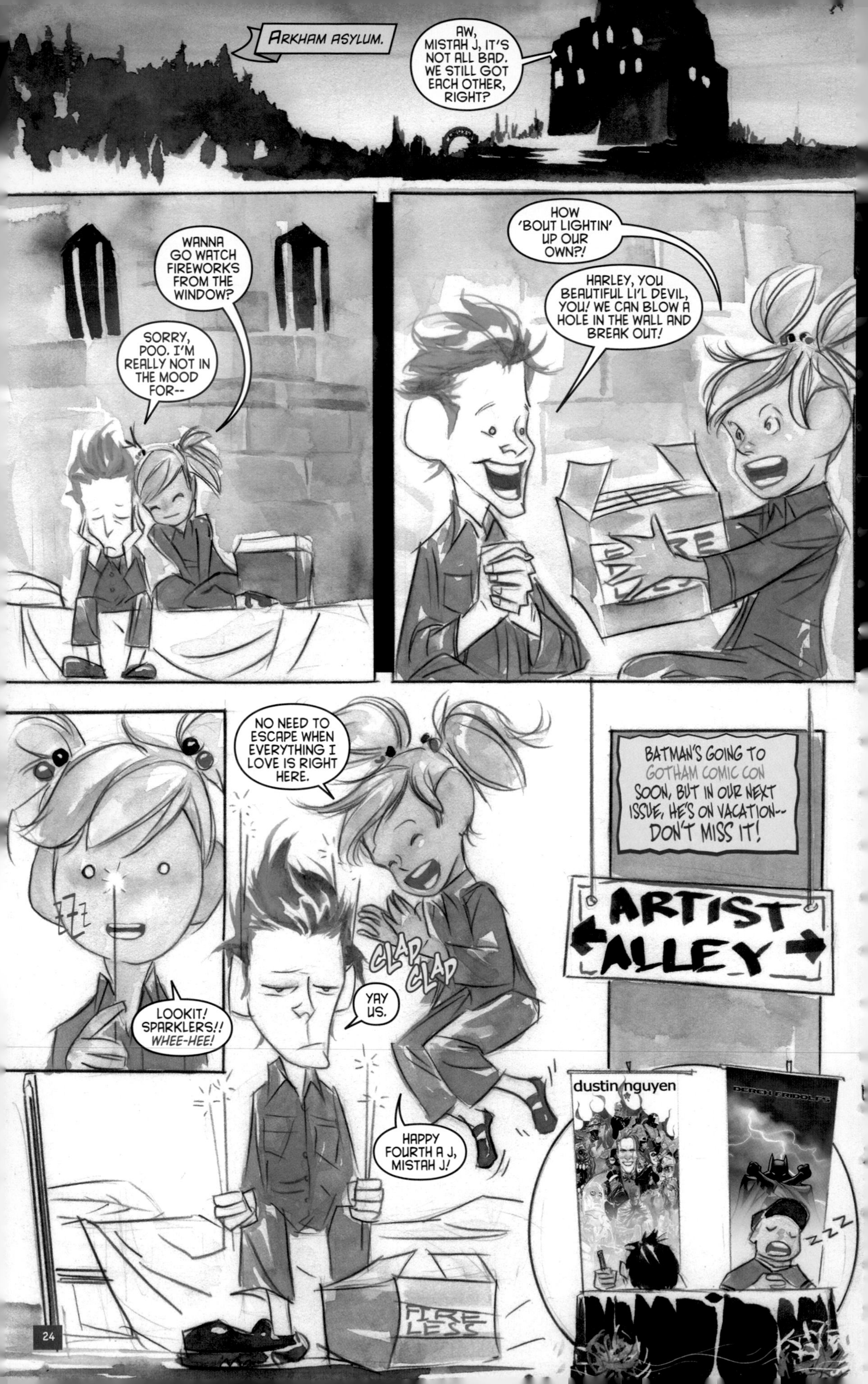
ARKHAM ASYLUM.
AW, MISTAH J, IT'S NOT ALL BAD. WE STILL GOT EACH OTHER, RIGHT?
WANNA GO WATCH FIREWORKS FROM THE WINDOW?
SORRY, POO. I'M REALLY NOT IN THE MOOD FOR--
HOW 'BOUT LIGHTIN' UP OUR OWN?!
HARLEY, YOU BEAUTIFUL LI'L DEVIL, YOU! WE CAN BLOW A HOLE IN THE WALL AND BREAK OUT!
NO NEED TO ESCAPE WHEN EVERYTHING I LOVE IS RIGHT HERE.
LOOKIT! SPARKLERS!! WHEE-HEE!
YAY US.
CLAP CLAP
HAPPY FOURTH A J, MISTAH J!
FIRE LESS
BATMAN'S GOING TO GOTHAM COMIC CON SOON, BUT IN OUR NEXT ISSUE, HE'S ON VACATION-- DON'T MISS IT!
ARTIST ALLEY
dustin nguyen
DEREK FRIDOLFS

CREATORS

DUSTIN NGUYEN — CO-WRITER & ILLUSTRATOR

Dustin Nguyen is an American comic artist whose body of work includes Wildcats v3.0, The Authority Revolution, Batman, Superman/Batman, Detective Comics, Batgirl, and his creator owned project Manifest Eternity. Currently, he produces all the art for Batman: Li'l Gotham, which is also written by himself and Derek Fridolfs. Outside of comics, Dustin moonlights as a conceptual artist for toys, games, and animation. In his spare time, he enjoys sleeping, driving, and sketching things he loves.

DEREK FRIDOLFS — CO-WRITER

Derek Fridolfs is a comic book writer, inker, and artist. He resides in Gotham--present and future.

GLOSSARY

arigato (ah-ree-GAH-toh)--arigato means "thank you" in Japanese

catastrophe (kuh-TASS-truh-fee)--a sudden and widespread disaster, or misfortune, mishap, or failure

compromised (KOM-pruh-mized)--if something is compromised, it has been exposed to danger or suspicion

cowl (KOWL)--a hooded garment or the hooded part of a garment

ecological (ee-koh-LAH-juh-kuhl)--tending to benefit or cause minimal damage to the environment

experimental (ek-spare-uh-MEN-tuhl)--something yet to be proven to be completely functional

inhabit (in-HAB-it)--to live or dwell in a place

obligatory (uh-BLIG-uh-tohr-ee)--required

rendezvous (RAHN-duh-voo)--an agreement by two parties to meet a specific time and place, or the place where two parties will meet

vast (VASST)--very great in size, degree, or proportions

VISUAL QUESTIONS & PROMPTS

1. Why is the Joker dressed this way? What does it have to do with his evil plan?

2. What reasons might Batman have to play chess with the Riddler?

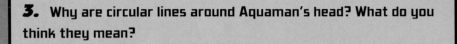

3. Why are circular lines around Aquaman's head? What do you think they mean?

4. What do you think the expression on the Joker's face means in this panel? How does he feel? Why does he feel that way?

BATMAN™
LI'L GOTHAM

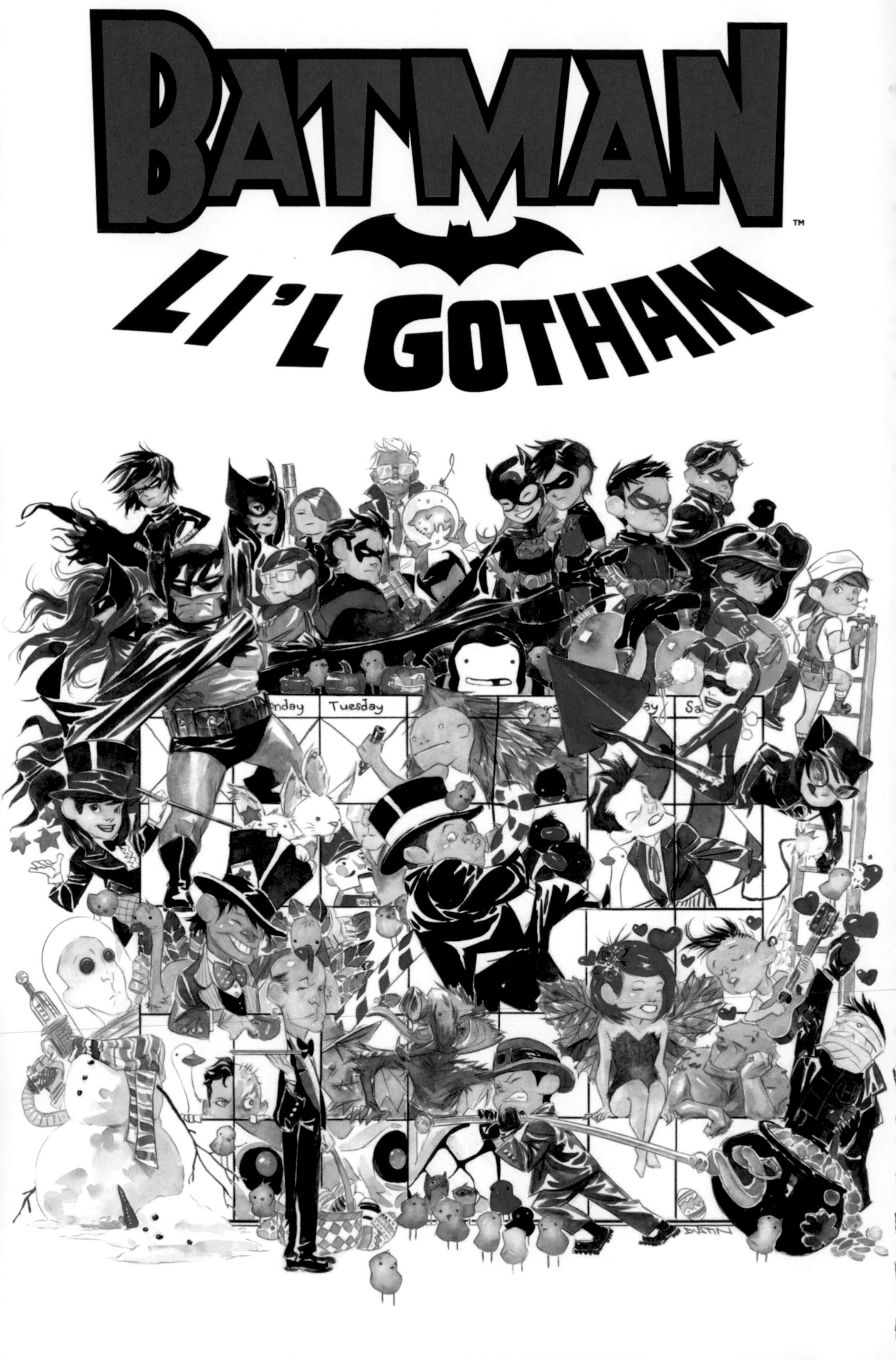

Tuesday

READ THEM ALL!

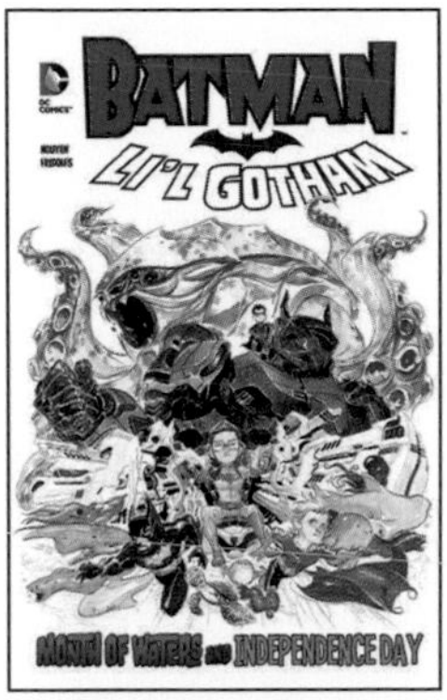
BATMAN
LI'L GOTHAM
MONTH OF WATERS AND INDEPENDENCE DAY

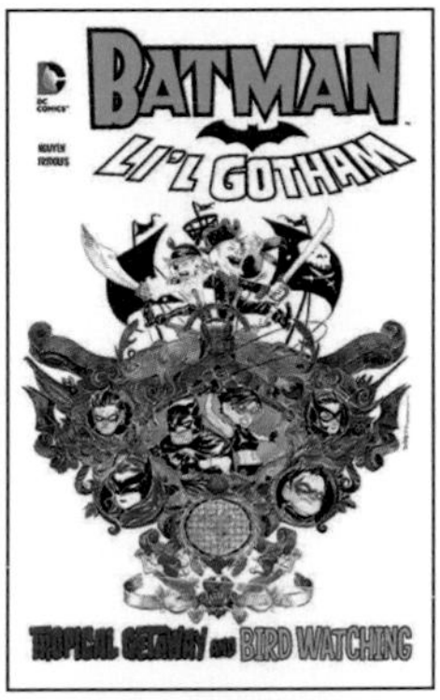
BATMAN
LI'L GOTHAM
TROPICAL GETAWAY AND BIRD WATCHING

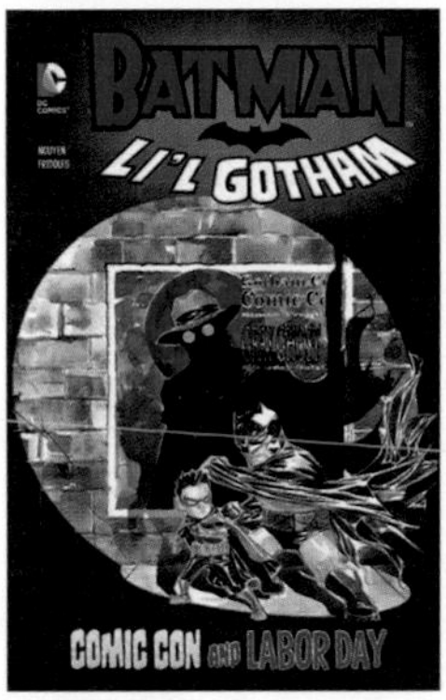
BATMAN
LI'L GOTHAM
COMIC CON AND LABOR DAY

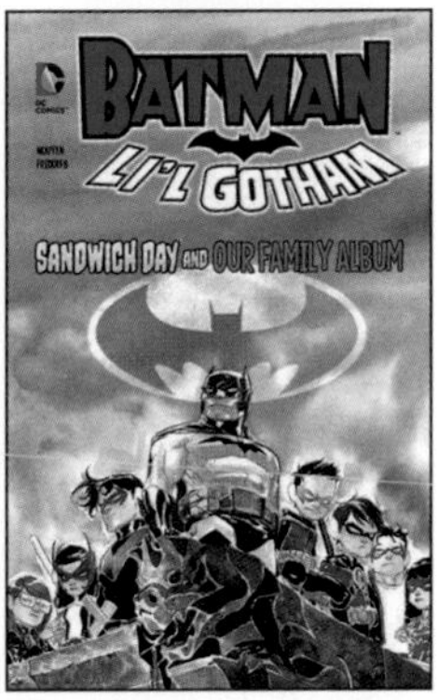
BATMAN
LI'L GOTHAM
SANDWICH DAY AND OUR FAMILY ALBUM

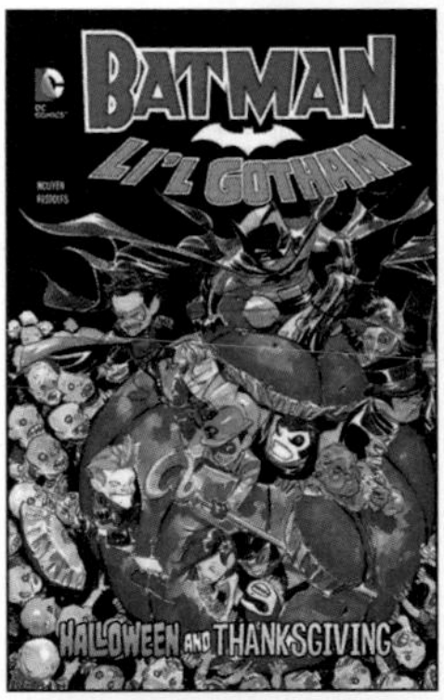
BATMAN
LI'L GOTHAM
HALLOWEEN AND THANKSGIVING

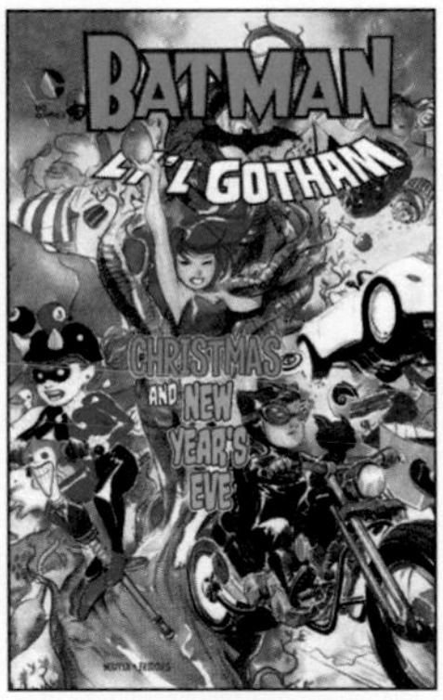
BATMAN
LI'L GOTHAM
CHRISTMAS AND NEW YEAR'S EVE

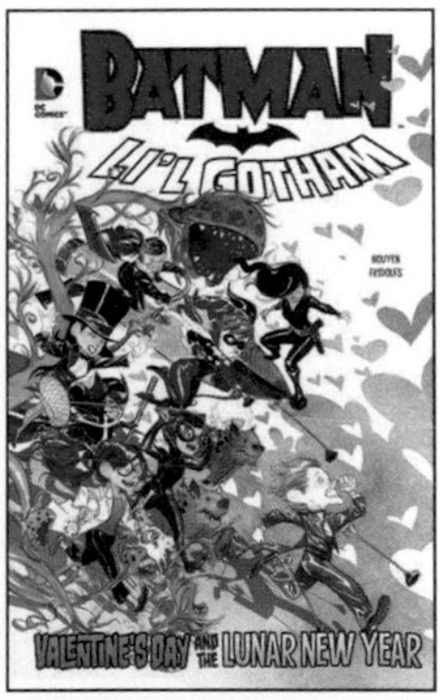
BATMAN
LI'L GOTHAM
VALENTINE'S DAY AND THE LUNAR NEW YEAR

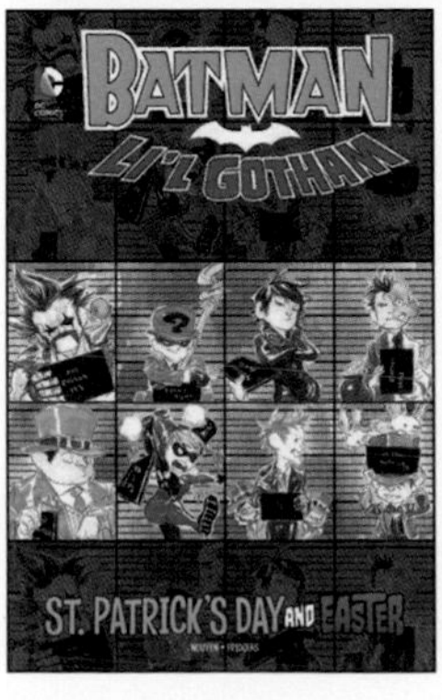
BATMAN
LI'L GOTHAM
ST. PATRICK'S DAY AND EASTER

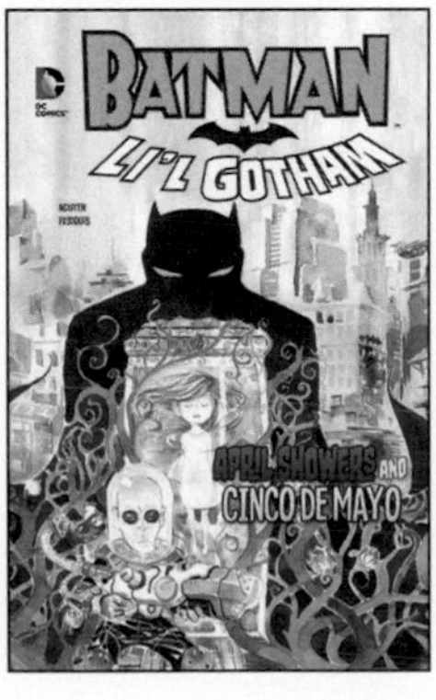
BATMAN
LI'L GOTHAM
APRIL SHOWERS AND CINCO DE MAYO

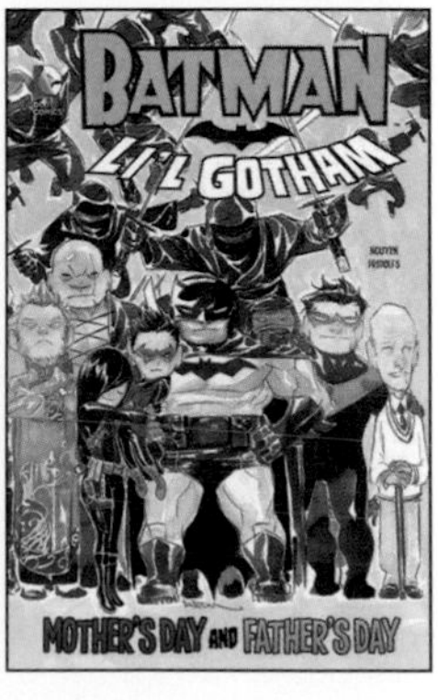
BATMAN
LI'L GOTHAM
MOTHER'S DAY AND FATHER'S DAY

BATMAN™ LI'L GOTHAM

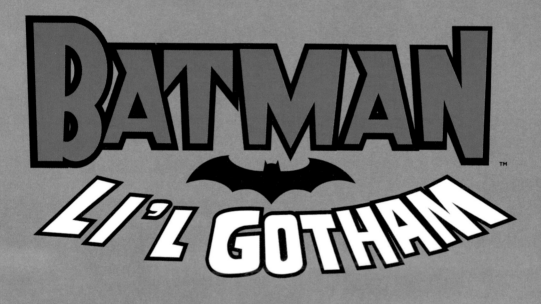